MEDITERRANEAN DATING GAME

SCARLET WILSON

ROMANCE

ISBN-13: 978-1-335-47081-2

Mediterranean Dating Game

For questions and comments about the quality of this book, please contact us at CustomerService@Harlequin.com.

Harlequin Enterprises ULC
22 Adelaide St. West, 41st Floor
Toronto, Ontario M5H 4E3, Canada
www.Harlequin.com

HarperCollins Publishers
Macken House, 39/40 Mayor Street Upper,
Dublin 1, D01 C9W8, Ireland
www.HarperCollins.com

Printed in U.S.A.

1 2 3 4 5 6 7 8 9 10 HDC 28 27 26 25

Scarlet Wilson wrote her first story aged eight and has never stopped. She's worked in the health service for more than thirty years, having trained as a nurse and a health visitor. Scarlet now works in public health and lives on the West Coast of Scotland with her fiancé and their two sons. Writing medical romances and contemporary romances is a dream come true for her.

Books by Scarlet Wilson

Harlequin Romance

Family Reunion in London

Christmas Surprise for Her Boss

Cinderella's Costa Rican Adventure
Slow Dance with the Italian

Harlequin Medical Romance

Christmas North and South

Melting Dr. Grumpy's Frozen Heart

Honolulu Medics

Hawaiian Kiss with the Brooding Doc

California Nurses

Nurse with a Billion Dollar Secret

Cinderella's Kiss with the ER Doc
Her Summer with the Brooding Vet
Nurse's Dubai Temptation

Visit the Author Profile page
at Harlequin.com for more titles.

To Sheila Hodgson, a wonderful editor
who has inspired, motivated and supported
Mills and Boon writers her whole career.
I am blessed and privileged to have known you x

"Okay, let's make a deal—one that will benefit us both."

Sydney let her raised eyebrows do the talking.

Vittorio filled the gap. "I'll be your date. If we say we're a couple, they'll leave us alone."

"And what do you get out of this?"

"Someone doesn't get to rush me into babies and marriage."

Sydney was instantly suspicious. "Sounds too good to be true. What else?"

"What do you mean?"

Her eyes swept the room. "How will it look if the Chief Exec joined in the love boat to get a date?"

"Maybe they'll just think I'm a fun guy?" he said, clearly reaching for the first thing he could think of.

Sydney leaned back. "Vittorio Conti, are you known as a fun guy?"

She watched as he contemplated the truth and sighed. "Not always."

"Not ever?"

It was Vittorio's turn to look around the room. "Do you really want to have to speed date every night with the guys you just met?"

"Probably not."

The choice was simple.

She swallowed, then lifted her glass towards him. "How bad can this be?"

Dear Reader,

Writing a cruise ship book is fun. Where else can you find a different destination every day, and throw lots of issues at your hero and heroine?

I've always secretly wanted to be Indiana Jones, so my female character, Sydney Scott, is absolutely based on him. Vittorio Conti, my Italian hero, is the last guy who would want to be roped into any kind of dating game, but that's what makes things so much fun.

I hope you enjoy this story as much as I do.

Scarlet Wilson

CHAPTER ONE

SYDNEY SCOTT STARED at her brother as she tried to process the words he'd just said. 'What?'

She listened as he spoke again. 'We did it as a surprise. It's been months since you've had a holiday, and Jess and I thought it would be good for you. I cleared it with Josef.'

She blinked. Josef. Her boss. He'd cleared her apparent 'holiday' with her boss. 'Why would you do that?'

She was aware that her voice had developed a chilly tone. But her brother knew her better than this.

She knew that Pete was beginning to regret his good idea as he started to stammer. 'Well… you know how it is…you have to clear holidays with the boss. And I told him that we were planning a family event.'

She pushed her fedora back from her damp brow. 'This doesn't sound like a family event.'

Pete pulled a face. 'It sounded good enough to get your holiday scheduled in.'

Sydney sat down on one of the nearby chairs. The edges of the large white tent flapped in the wind. It kept off the heat, but the sand was in virtually every pore of her body. She'd been on this Egyptian archaeological dig for the past eight months. They were searching for a lost tomb of one of the lesser-known pharaohs. If this were a game of hide-and-seek, the pharaoh would absolutely be winning.

They'd found and catalogued a mountain of wonderful artefacts. She started every day with that little feeling in her stomach, that today could be *that* day. The day they finally found something spectacular. She'd dreamed of this since she was a child and had first heard about Egypt, pyramids and pharaohs.

'I don't need you to book me a holiday, Pete. I'm not a child. And I'm not your responsibility.'

As soon as the words left her mouth she regretted them as a frown creased his brow. He sighed and dug his hands into his pockets. 'You know I promised Mum I'd look out for you, and make sure you weren't working too hard.'

Now her stomach clenched. Yes, she did know that. 'I'm an adult, Pete. I can arrange and book my own holidays.'

Pete gave her the dead eye. That's what she'd called it since they were children. When he reached the point that he was clearly tired of trying to reason with her and started to switch off to her arguments.

'Jess packed your case,' he continued.

'She…what?' Now Sydney was incredulous. Who packed someone else's case? How on earth would they know what she would want to take on holiday?

He shrugged. 'Case is in the car. And we better leave now, as I've heard some flights are getting cancelled.'

'What? Why?' For a few seconds she was momentarily distracted by the news.

'Something about Pompeii.'

Sydney stopped dead. She'd spent years studying archaeology before finally specialising in Egyptology. But anything in the field at all sparked her interest. 'Oh no,' said Pete, wagging his finger at her. 'Don't even think about it.'

She looked down at her clothes, her khaki working trousers and loose white shirt—with a few definite smudges—'I need to get changed.'

'No time,' said Pete with a wave of his hand, as Josef appeared at the entrance to the large tent.

'It worked.' Josef smiled broadly, clearly enjoying being a conspirator with her brother.

Sydney glared at him. 'Was this your idea?'

His smile stayed fixed in place. 'No, but as your employer, I am legally obliged to make sure you take your holidays, so Pete just saved me the fights and hassle with you.'

'What's happening at Pompeii?' She couldn't help herself.

Josef shook his head. 'Nothing. Just worry about reaching your destination.'

Frustrated, Sydney pulled her fedora from her head, freeing her dark curls. 'Why won't anyone tell me what's going on? Surely I have a right to know if you're taking me to the airport, and flights are being cancelled?'

Pete gave a short nod. 'Okay, I'll tell you in the car.'

There was a long silence before Sydney finally let out a sigh. 'Okay.' She picked up her notebook from a table and pressed it into Josef's hands. 'Everything is up to date and catalogued. Bernie is currently supervising the students. None of them have given any cause for concern.' She gave a little smile. 'And a few are showing real promise. I think you'll like them.'

Every year they were inundated with requests from students, and individuals around the world who would love to be a part of any of the archaeological digs in Egypt. She'd been lucky enough to get on two digs herself as a student, and that was how she'd first met her mentor, Josef.

While the application process was easy, the interviews were tough. And Sydney took pride in identifying those who were genuinely interested and invested, those who thought it might look interesting on a CV, and those who were applying on a whim. The final group of wannabe fortune or treasure hunters were not even worth discussing, and always ended up in the disregarded pile.

Digs weren't glamourous. They were hard work, in a range of temperatures that were at best unpleasant and at worst unbearable. And that was to say nothing of the wind, and the sand. Who knew that those tiny grains could be so irritating?

Something pooled deep inside. She really didn't want to leave. She wanted to stay here and keep exploring next to her Egyptian counterparts. What if they made a major discovery when she wasn't here?

She turned to face Pete again. 'You know, you've sprung this on me. I haven't had time to prepare. I need to do a proper handover with Josef, and brief all the students on their duties for the next week.'

But Josef broke in. 'Sydney, you are the most organised person I've ever worked with—in fact, you're so organised you're scary sometimes. Everything is up to date. The holiday is arranged. Go.'

She hesitated again, and for the first time in months acknowledged how much her bones were aching. She couldn't remember the last time she'd gotten a proper night's sleep, usually because her brain was buzzing with all the things to do the next day, or on admin tasks related to the dig.

Would a week of lying somewhere in the sun really be so bad?

Pete walked over and nudged her elbow. 'Come on. Don't want to have to do that run-through-the-airport thing.'

Josef bent over and kissed her on the cheek. 'Send a photograph of the sights,' he said.

She frowned, scribbling a few other notes and handing them to one of the students who'd just come inside. 'Give these to Bernie,' she said, grabbing her hat and sticking it back on her head.

The wind was already picking up as they headed to her brother's car and she lowered her head, letting the brim of her hat take the worst of the sand as she clambered into her brother's car. Sure enough, her suitcase was in the rear seat.

'What's wrong with the trunk?' she asked Pete.

He gave her a noncommittal smile. 'Oh, there's one in the trunk too.' He started the engine and pulled down the site road, back towards the desert road.

'Why on earth would I need two suitcases? Who takes two suitcases on holiday?'

'I left the packing to Jess,' he said, clearly not trying to engage.

Sydney pulled her hat from her head again and plunked it in her lap, ignoring the sand pouring onto her trousers. 'Exactly what kind of a holiday is this?' She pulled down the sun visor in the car, then something else struck her. 'And it is just for a week, isn't it?'

'Maybe a fortnight,' he said, keeping his eyes on the road.

'What?' It came out as kind of a screech.

'It's okay, you know it's cleared with Josef.'

She pointed to her chest. 'But it's not cleared with me, Pete. Why on earth didn't you talk to me about this?' She could feel her anger building and couldn't believe she'd actually got into the car.

'I tried to—on a number of occasions. But you never have time—or you say you never have time. I keep trying to work out what's wrong that you can't give yourself any down time, or spend time with your family.'

She froze, not wanting to acknowledge the words he'd said, instant dismissals coming to her lips but not forming actual words between them.

'Jess and I have tried to meet up with you six times since Christmas.' He shot her a glance. 'Every time you've made an excuse.'

She shifted uncomfortably in the car seat.

'I'm...just busy,' she said, knowing how feeble it sounded.

'I miss her too,' he said, and left the words just hanging there in the air.

An instant lump formed in her throat.

Her brother continued. 'I don't know if seeing me and Jess reminds you of her, or if there's another reason you don't want to be around us. But this isn't just about you, Sydney. She was my mother too. She treated Jess like another daughter. We miss her every day. We're grieving too.'

Although she swallowed, the lump stayed firmly in place. 'I know,' she managed, fixing her eyes on the landscape rather than on her brother.

The silence was uncomfortable, and Sydney was immediately full of regrets. The first one being that she'd actually got into this car with her brother...followed by the fact that what he was saying was likely true.

Work was easy. It was easy to get lost in. To stay enthusiastic about. She'd once laid a bet with a group of fellow students that the two most random things that people would say they were interested in—if given a list—were dinosaurs and Egypt.

Someone had actually written down a random list and gone around the pub they were in, coming back with a puzzled face, asking how she could possibly know that. 'People are curious creatures,' she'd replied. 'It's the intrigue. The unknown, and the possible secrets around both subjects.'

Even though that had been a few years ago, she still felt it was true. People were naturally curious about Egypt. Everyone knew just a little about it. Some facts, some popular myths.

Indiana Jones had made archaeology seem sexy and action packed, and people always liked to imagine themselves in that sort of role.

Depending on who was asking, Sydney sometimes told them about the hours and hours of research, the around eighty thousand artefacts still to be catalogued at the Egyptian Museum of Cairo, and the fact it was estimated only about half of the tombs of known pharaohs had been found.

If the person annoyed her, she told them about the relentless sun and sandstorms, the biting wind, the unusually cold nights, and the digging for hours and hours, days and days, months and months with no huge success. That tended to stop their imaginary starring role in the next big movie.

'A holiday might be nice,' she said, as a conciliatory move. 'Are you going to tell me where I'm going yet?'

She was contemplating a large beach parasol,

a sun lounger, plenty of sunscreen, a cocktail, and a good book.

'You're going lots of places.'

Her head spun so rapidly she must have looked like a horror movie character. 'What?'

He actually had a hint of a smile on his face. 'You're going on a cruise.'

'A cruise?' She repeated the words as if she were trying to make sure she'd heard him correctly.

He gave her a quick glance. 'Yep, a cruise. A chance to see a whole host of destinations, Barcelona, Venice, Sicily, Croatia, Monte Carlo, Rome, Mykonos, Santorini. Plus, a few days at sea. You'll get to see everything.'

Sydney started to feel a warm heat rise inside her. A cruise ship. In the middle of the sea. Trapped, with all those people—perfect strangers.

Panic spread across her chest. 'When did I ever say I wanted to go on a cruise? What if it's like *Titanic* and they don't have enough lifeboats for everyone? What if I fall overboard? What if people try to play friends with me and I have to play hide-and-seek for the next fortnight to escape from them?' She tugged at the loose collar of her shirt. 'I don't remember ever saying I wanted to go on a cruise.' Her mouth felt very dry.

'Don't be such a worry wart,' her brother

shot at her. He was laughing now. 'I tell you that you're going on a luxury cruise all around the Med and will visit gorgeous cities, and you immediately jump to falling off the boat, not enough lifeboats, and avoiding people—although that one—' he rolled his eyes at her '—doesn't exactly take me by surprise.'

Sydney let out a long slow breath, trying not to let the sensations of panic overwhelm her. Part of his words gave her a jolt. She wrinkled her nose and looked at him. 'Worry wart?'

His smile softened. 'Mum used to say it all the time. It reminds me of her. I like to use it.'

Her tight shoulders relaxed back into the car seat, and she gave a soft smile. 'So she did. I don't think I've heard it since…'

Pete reached over and squeezed her hand. It was the briefest of touches. They weren't really that kind of family, but she appreciated it.

'I'm still not sure about a cruise,' she said.

'What's the worst that can happen?' he replied automatically, then lifted one hand off the wheel. 'No, in fact, don't. Don't say it.'

'Well, I've covered the falls and the lifeboats, so I guess the only thing left is that disease where the whole ship has to spend the whole time in their cabins because everyone is being sick.'

'It won't happen. This is the maiden voyage

of this cruise ship. It's a brand-new, state-of-the-art Italian cruise liner. They even have crystals in the stairs in the main atrium.'

'Is it still an atrium if it's on a ship?'

He shot her another glance as he started indicating towards the exit. 'Would anyone but you care?'

'Probably the ship people,' she said.

He wagged his finger at her. 'See, you don't even know what they're called. Think of this as a new expedition. A learning experience. You don't know anything about ships and the sea. This could open up a whole new world for you.'

'At the bottom of the sea?' Her sharp gaze met his and he sighed.

'I'll make a deal with you.'

She sat straighter, immediately intrigued. 'What deal?'

'If you go on this cruise and hate it, you can pick the destination for my and Jess's next holiday, but only if you stick this out to the end.'

The smile spread instantly across Sydney's face. 'I can send you both anywhere, and you'll go?'

She knew Pete would be regretting those words instantly, and would have a hard time explaining to Jess why they might end up somewhere unusual and likely unpleasant.

She held out her hand to him. 'Pete Scott, you've got yourself a deal.'

* * *

The chief purser and cruise director had their heads together and were talking in low voices.

Vittorio Conti could sniff a conspiracy at twenty paces. 'What's going on?'

There was tension in the air. The maiden voyage of his newest cruise liner, the *Minerva*, was due to take place in the next few hours. But it seemed that the Roman gods had other plans for him, and Mount Vesuvius had decided to release some volcanic ash to such an extent that flights had been cancelled across parts of Italy.

The ship had that first-sail buzz about it as staff hurried to make sure everything was in place and last-minute details were being finalised.

The chief purser, Moretti, looked at him. 'We've been notified that several of our guests will not arrive in time, or maybe at all.'

Jen the cruise director's normally tanned skin looked pale. 'This will interfere with our numbers. We had an expectation of the same number of males and females attending. Right now, we are skewed significantly.'

Vittorio took a deep breath. He'd hated this concept from the start. But the board had approved the maiden voyage of the *Minerva* to jump on the bandwagon of all the biggest TV shows, *Married at First Sight*, *The Bachelor*, and *Love Island*, to have a cruise specifically designed for single people who want to find their perfect match.

There were counsellors, dating experts, Instagram influencers, and reporters all on board to help with the publicity. An Italian TV station had also sent along a TV crew to capture some footage.

The schedule Jen had put together was—in Vittorio's eyes—terrifying. A round of three-minute speed dating was the first event, followed by impromptu questions where couples would be matched based on their answers.

Instead of the normal tours at the ports, most were arranged for couples or groups of four. If you wanted to get off at the port, you had to pitch to a partner.

Vittorio tried to be open-minded. If you'd come on board, knowing the purpose of this cruise and how it was scheduled, it could work out well. Jen had assured him that all participants had been sent the information. But pulling people in at the last moment? It could be disaster.

'We can't cancel,' he said in low voice. 'There's too much riding on this.'

Moretti blinked. 'Well, we need to find some men. What about some of the crew?'

Jen groaned. 'We set up criteria at the beginning. Obviously, and most importantly, everyone had to be single. They had to either have reached a certain education level, have a job within a wage bracket, or a company with a certain yearly turnover.'

Vittorio rolled his eyes, and she shot back immediately, 'You think all the other shows don't have criteria which have to be followed? This isn't just any dating experience. This is an exclusive, and expensive—' she added, raising her eyebrows '—cruise, where you could meet an intellectual equal, or a person who has the same entrepreneurial spirit as you. We have to live up to that promise.'

She glanced at her watch and looked at them both.

'I suggest if you have any available friends, you start calling them. Otherwise, I'm going down to the port to try to use my persuasion techniques to get some locals on board.'

Somcthing flashed across her eyes.

'Actually, one of the male Instagrammers said he'd wished he'd known earlier. I might try him.'

She disappeared into the throng of staff and out of sight.

Vittorio turned back to Moretti. 'How long do we have?'

He glanced at the clock above the check-in counter. 'How long until the passengers arrive?'

Moretti sighed. 'Some are already in the terminal dropping their luggage off.'

Vittorio couldn't help but run his fingers through his short hair. 'I guess we better start phoning friends then?' he said, before striding off to his office.

The place was buzzing, and not at all like she'd expected. Sydney had dropped her two cases at the cruise terminal and tried to take a deep breath, but the noise was incredible. People were clearly excited about being here.

Her flight had circled the airport twice before finally landing, and as she'd waited to be collected at arrivals, she'd realised just how many flights had been cancelled.

When she'd landed at Marco Polo Airport in Venice, she hadn't even have time to get a glimpse of the beautiful city before she'd been escorted to a bus that transferred her to the Venice Cruise Terminal, where most of the main cruises departed from.

Weren't cruises supposed to be for pensioners? She couldn't really see anyone around pension age, and there weren't any children either. Were they banned from cruise ships? She wasn't exactly sure. All she could see was a range of people like her, in their twenties or thirties. It seemed a bit…off.

She moved to the area to present her boarding pass and passport, and to have her photo taken before she boarded the ship. Someone checked her hand luggage and gave her a cruise card with the instruction that she would need it to exit and enter the ship at the ports.

Finally, she was shown where she could board the boat, and she took a few moments to appreciate the ship from the outside.

Standing next to the hull, the actual size took her by surprise. She had a quick check online. Swimming pools, cocktail bars, shops, a theatre, a spa, a cinema, seven different places to eat, a gym, tennis and badminton courts, and an executive centre. It wasn't the biggest cruise liner that had ever existed, but the emphasis was on quality and the experience that it delivered. At least that's what the promise was.

Sydney gave a surprising shudder. Was she nervous? Was it anticipation? She'd never cruised before. If there were rules, she didn't know them. Did you tip on a cruise ship? Did you have to dress for dinner every night?

She could hear her brother's voice almost echoing in her head. *There's only one way to find out.*

She took a deep breath and stepped up to board. Everything went smoothly, she was shown into the main entrance and up some stairs to the check-in area. There was a deluge of uniformed professional staff, directing travellers, handing out maps of the boat, and pointing to information about the ship's itinerary. But all of that was lost to Sydney. Because right now, she couldn't see past the gigantic purple, pink and gold sign. *Welcome to the Love Boat!*

The what? This had to some kind of joke. Wasn't that some ancient TV show that had been popular before she was even born? She was still standing in stunned silence when an immaculate woman in a navy-and-white uniform approached her. 'Welcome to the *Minerva*, my name is Claudia. We are so glad you've joined us for our very special maiden voyage. We have welcome drinks and snacks in the restaurant just around the corner. If you think you've left anything behind, we have a whole host of shops in the deck below. Can I direct you to your room? Or maybe you would like to explore a little?'

Sydney was frozen in shock. Her eyes started to flit around more sceptically. Yes, there did seem to be a remarkable amount of single passengers. Some were already chatting to each other. Did everyone else know about this? Was she the only person who didn't?

She gestured to the sign. 'The love boat—what exactly does that mean?'

She realised immediately how clipped her

words must have been by Claudia's reaction. But Sydney Scott wasn't sorry. She was at the end of her tether—and that tether was currently a very short rope.

Claudia's perfect forehead showed a little crease. 'It was in all the publicity materials,' she said warily, showing her perfect teeth. 'The *Minerva*'s maiden voyage is also a cruise for singles. A chance to meet your perfect partner while cruising the Mediterranean and visiting some of the most romantic places in the world.'

Sydney's heart sank like a stone. She'd already had reservations about the cruise. But a love boat? That was absolutely the last place on earth she wanted to be.

Her first boyfriend had rented out her room at university when Sydney had gone on her first dig—and then he'd fallen in love with his new roommate, leaving Sydney heartbroken and homeless.

Her second serious relationship had ended when Chris had gone to 'find' himself. Ten years on, she'd no idea where he'd gone, or what he'd found.

Finally, Rob, her former fiancé, had been the biggest cliché of the bunch and fallen for his secretary. They were now happily married with a baby on the way.

Sydney had pretty much sworn off men for

life. The only men she was interested in were those that were dead and buried in Egyptian sands.

'It's not compulsory to join in, is it?' she asked, her stomach giving a flip as if it already knew the answer.

Claudia looked even more confused. 'It's the whole purpose of the cruise. There are photographers and vloggers here to capture the fun of the maiden voyage—to let the world know how the maiden voyage of the love boat is going.'

'But if someone didn't feel up to it…or was unwell,' she added hopefully.

'Ma'am, if you feel unwell, I can take you to our medical centre. We have a doctor and two nurses and offer twenty-four-hour emergency care if required. Are you feeling unwell?' She gently put her hand on Sydney's arm.

Sydney shook her head. The noise around them was amplifying as more and more people were boarding. Most looked happy, even excited to be here.

'This just…isn't what I expected it to be,' said Sydney, raising her voice to be heard. 'I just expected a cruise—a normal cruise. Not a—' she gestured at the sign '—love boat. That's not for me. I don't want to be part of this.' She turned her head, looking rapidly about the place for any kind of escape route just as a loud funnel sounded.

'Can I just disembark? I don't want to be on the love boat.' It came out as almost a shout.

Claudia's eyes widened, and she shook her head. 'I'm sorry, ma'am. That noise signifies we've just set sail.' She seemed set on trying to placate her. 'Why don't you collect a cocktail and go and watch the boat leave port. Most people enjoy it. You'll get a great view if you go upstairs.'

Vittorio could feel the sweat gather around his collar. 'Tell me you got enough men?' he said to Jen.

She was looking flustered, and that was unusual. Jen had been on the roughest of seas, with furniture that wasn't nailed to the floor flying around her, and still looked like the calmest person in the room. Her hair had started to unravel from her sleek bun, her jacket was undone, and her shirt was coming untucked from its usual neat position.

She swallowed and looked at him. Her voice was odd. 'I can guarantee we have exactly equal numbers of eligible people on board.'

He blinked. 'What's the but?' He knew there was one. He could hear it in her voice.

Her eyes drifted down to the very expensive

carpet that lined the office floor. 'One of them is you.'

'What?' He stood up, pushing both hands down on the desk.

She shot him a pleading glance. 'You said to phone friends, but not all of them were available. Some were in other parts of the country with no chance of a flight getting here in time.'

'Surely you can rustle up another man from somewhere?'

She pulled a face. 'I already have. Two, actually.'

'Who?' Now his stomach was turning uneasily.

She squeezed her eyes closed. 'Jon Moretti the purser, and Evan Reid, the classical pianist on board.'

Vittorio didn't know whether to laugh or cry. Jon would be just as horrified as he was. Evan was a gentle soul, definitely single, and usually pursued by half of the passengers on a normal cruise. He might take it better than the rest of them.

The ship gave a soft judder that he instantly recognised as the first pull out of port. He'd only intended to see the passengers board; he'd never had any intention of being here for the entire cruise. As the executive chairman of the company, he was never usually down at grass roots level. But for the launch of the new cruise ship, one which would be the flagship of their fleet, he'd wanted to make sure everything went without a hitch.

He was now seeing the flaw in this plan.

'This could be good for you,' said Jen, giving him a hopeful glance.

'What do you mean?'

She pulled a face, obviously feeling a bit awkward. 'You had some bad publicity in the past. Maybe, if you're seen taking part in this, it could soften your image, make you seem more approachable.'

He could feel himself bristle but told himself not to react. The bad publicity had been a misunderstanding—one he hadn't felt like explaining to the world at the expense of someone else, so he'd borne the brunt of it. It wasn't easy having part of your life under the looking glass of the world, but Jen had a point. This could be beneficial. For him, and for the cruise ship's publicity.

'As long as things are done professionally and the cameras are kept at arm's length,' he said quickly, before he had too much time to think about it, and could list one hundred reasons how this could all go wrong.

'Done.' She smiled quickly, clearly agreeing before he changed his mind.

His office door was open and in amongst the

throng of people he could hear a raised voice. His feet took him automatically to the door. There was a woman, dark curly hair, a strange hat in one hand, dressed in a white shirt and khaki pants. It took him a few moments to register what seemed oddly familiar about the outfit. She reminded him of a female version of Indiana Jones.

She was clearly trying to contain herself but looked irate. Claudia, one of their most accomplished members of staff, was trying to placate her. Jen joined him at his side and they both heard a few snippets of the conversation.

I shouldn't be here.

This isn't my kind of cruise.

Is there any other way off this boat?

Vittorio sighed. 'This is going to be a disaster.'

Jen gave him a glance. 'Actually, maybe not. Looks like someone else has been blindsided by the love cruise. She might be the perfect person to pair you with to keep you out of the clutches of any internet-savvy influencer who might figure out who you are and want to report back on you.'

'You think that might happen?'

'Well, it will if I tell them.'

He sighed. He was watching the interaction between the woman and Claudia with interest.

He could read the familiar expression on her face when she realised the ship had set sail and she couldn't escape. For a second, he thought he might laugh, then realised how unprofessional that would be.

She was a beauty. Without a doubt. He wasn't too sure about the clothes, but he'd heard people from some fandoms liked to dress up. Maybe that's what she was doing. Her skin was lightly tanned, and her dark curls were wild, cascading down her back. It was clear she had a passionate nature—and right now that passion was aimed at getting off his ship, which wasn't exactly meant to be the plan.

He shook his head. 'Don't you dare pair me with her. She looks as if she's ready to kill someone. The last we thing need is a murder on board the maiden voyage of the *Minerva*. No one would set foot on her again.'

He watched as the woman stuck some strands of curly hair behind one ear with a slightly panicked gaze.

He nudged Jen. 'But upgrade her to the executive suite. At least that way if she's upset and angry we can keep an eye on her and try to wow her with the facilities and service on the boat.'

Jen gave him a curious look. 'So, keep the potential murderer where we can watch her?' She smiled. 'You're the boss.'

And she disappeared out into the flurry of guests before he had a chance to say anything else.

CHAPTER TWO

SYDNEY WAS STILL trying to capture her breath as she was led to her cabin. There seemed to have been some quiet chat around her as she'd been taken to another level and her luggage was transported.

The first things she noticed as they swung open her cabin door in the executive section of the ship was the space and the view. She looked at the new woman next to her, who'd introduced herself as Jen.

'This is enormous.' She walked inside the elegant room. 'Aren't cruise ship cabins supposed to be small?'

Jen beamed. 'This is an executive cabin. Larger than the regular size, with your own living room, bedroom, and balcony with Jacuzzi. You also have your own butler who can assist you with any needs that you may have. Cocktails, room service, any bookings you want to make around the ship.' She pointed to a leather-covered folder. 'All the details are in here, and

Javier—who is your butler—will help you with anything at all.'

Sydney was still pacing the room and marvelling at the size. The last hotel room she'd been in hadn't been this big, and it hadn't been floating on top of the ocean.

She walked over to the large glass doors and pulled them back, letting in a stiff, warm breeze that made the large cream curtains flutter. Sydney leaned forward, putting her hands on the balcony and taking in the view in front of her. They'd barely left port, but her view was of the expanse of wide ocean in front of her. It was slightly terrifying. Was this really the time to hear the *Jaws* theme tune in her head? Oh, her brother, Pete, would just love that.

The balcony was enclosed, completely private unless they were alongside some equally magnificent cruise ship in another port. The Jacuzzi faced towards the sea and had a handy table alongside for any of the aforementioned cocktails.

Jen followed her outside. 'Don't worry, Javier is already unpacking your suitcases for you.'

Sydney spun around, instantly aghast at the thought of someone seeing all her personal items—and then she realised she hadn't even packed these cases. She didn't have a single clue what either of them contained. Would Jess even have remembered to pack half the things she might need, not least her moisturiser and hair balm to stop her curls frizzing?

She resisted the temptation to go in and interfere, and instead took a deep breath. 'Did my brother really book me this room?'

Something flickered across Jen's face. 'We saw you were upset earlier, and thought an executive upgrade might make things more comfortable for you.'

In her head, Sydney was already contemplating just staying in this luxurious cabin for the next fourteen days. She didn't really need to visit the ports—did she?

But even that thought made her archaeological brain whirr. Would she really not take the chance to see the Colosseum again, or Katakolon and the site of the original Olympics? What about Santorini, with its view from the cliffs of the surrounding islands and all thc mythology that went alongside? Did this cruise visit Crete, with the opportunity to visit Knossos with the ancient maze and history of the labyrinth and Minotaur?

'Do you have an itinerary for the ship? I didn't get a chance to see it in advance.'

Jen pointed to a desk just inside the glass doors. 'Your itinerary for the ship's journey, and for the next fortnight, is included in the information on the desk.'

Javier was moving at lightning speed, hanging garments and sliding things into drawers as if he knew automatically where she might want to put everything.

But it struck Sydney that one key thing might be missing for this holiday. 'Is there a library on board?'

If Jen was surprised she didn't say anything, but instead showed Sydney a copy of the map of the ship, pointing out the library just beyond the check-in desks she'd been at earlier. 'There's plenty of new and classic books. I'm sure you'll find something that will interest you.'

'And internet?' asked Sydney.

'You'll connect automatically to the *Minerva* servers. You just have to agree to the standard conditions about your usage.' She gave the smallest smile. 'Coverage can, on occasion, be spotty. But we have a massive amount of content on the ship's TV channels. I'm sure you'll find something to keep you entertained.' She waved her hand at the giant flat-screen TV against the wall and facing the bed.

Sydney decided not to say anything at the thought of having a spotty internet connection. She suddenly pictured the ship in the dead of the night, in a dark ocean, with no way of contacting anyone, anywhere. Like one of the best horror movies. She shivered, then actually let out a laugh.

Where on earth were these random thoughts coming from? It's not like she'd ever been on a cruise before to have had a bad experience.

'You know what?' She smiled at Jen. 'I think I might take you up on the offer of a cocktail. Can I have a mai tai, please?'

'Absolutely.' Jen beamed. 'It will be here in a matter of minutes. Can I offer you some snacks too?'

'Why not,' said Sydney. *In for a penny, in for a pound.* It was another of her mother's old sayings and instantly sprang to mind.

Jen gave her a wave, and Javier was already stowing her cases with everything packed away. 'I'll see you tonight at six.' Jen smiled without giving any more details.

Sydney's eyes flicked to the folder and she shook her head. That could wait. Instead, she pulled her phone from her pocket. They'd barely left land so she'd still have a partial signal. She typed a text to her brother. The love boat? I WILL MAKE YOU PAY!

Vittorio finished the executive call with a colleague in New York and looked up. Jen was standing in the doorway.

He wasn't used to working like this—then again, he wasn't usually on one of his cruise liners. He was used to working from his penthouse office in Florence or his business address in Venice. At both of those venues he had impeccable personal assistants who held all calls and messages, and only approached when he gestured to them.

As a boy his mother had called him easily distracted. She might have been right. Because Vittorio preferred silence around him. No voices. No clicking of computer keys. No telephones ringing. The work that Vittorio could cover in a couple of hours of silence would take most normal people a full day. So, a cruise ship with constant noise and people interrupting was just about his worst-case scenario.

'What?' he said to Jen, trying not to sound rude, but wanting to get on.

'You're needed,' she said, her tone firm.

'For what?'

She raised her eyebrows. 'You have half an hour to get ready and present yourself at the ballroom for your scheduled speed-dating round.'

He groaned and shook his head. 'Can't you juggle the numbers, move other people around?' He pointed to a board on the wall. 'I know you're not letting all the eligible passengers do this at once. Give someone else an extra shot.'

She shook her head. 'We will not cheat anyone out of what they were promised on this cruise. Even numbers. Equal chances.'

He sighed. 'Are you going to even tell me what I have to do?'

'You have to freshen yourself up, change your clothes, and meet me at the ballroom.' She glanced at her watch. 'In exactly twenty-eight minutes. Now, move.'

The mai tai had actually been delightful. And it seemed that Jess knew her better than she'd thought. She'd packed some beautiful evening wear, plenty of light shirts and trousers for exploring cities, hats, sunglasses, and even some swimwear.

Sydney had pulled out a red long dress with bright embroidery and some black flat shoes. She'd washed her hair and left it with its normal dark curls. Jess had packed her straighteners, but Sydney only used them on occasion and didn't see the point. Although she was scheduled to attend an event, she wasn't out to impress anyone.

As she exited the cabin, there was almost a buzz in the air. She could see groups of people talking excitedly. People checking their reflections in any possible surface. As she neared the ballroom, the volume increased.

There were people with cameras, and others

livestreaming on their devices. Maybe the internet wasn't so spotty after all?

A waiter was standing with a large tray of cocktails. Sydney spotted the mai tai straight away, and decided she might as well take another. As she wandered into the ballroom, she saw a huge number of small tables with a chair at either side.

The itinerary that Jen had left hadn't specified what this event was. Sydney had presumed it would just be some welcome drinks. But it seemed she should have known better.

As if Jen could feel the vibes emanating from Sydney, she appeared on the stage in front of them. 'Welcome, everyone, to our first fun event!'

Applause sounded around the room. Everyone else seemed delighted to be there.

'This is a traditional speed-dating round. A quick way to break the ice and get a chance to get to know some of your fellow passengers. We have five hundred eligible men and women on board, all looking for love, or some kind of connection. We've broken you all into smaller groups to try to help keep the noise down. We're going to start simple. All men, please take a seat at one of the numbered tables. That's it. Pick your table now, please.'

There was a low hum as most of men moved

to the tables enthusiastically. Sydney did notice a little hesitation from a few, including a tall man in a dark suit. He looked as if he would pay good money to be anywhere but here. Much like she would.

He had that usual Mediterranean tanned skin, broad shoulders, and a bit of a scowl. She almost laughed out loud. He clasped his hands in front of him and looked around the room. Was he looking for the nearest exit?

Sydney took a sip of her mai tai. This might actually be amusing.

Jen kept talking as she stood in front of the largest glass bowl in the world. It looked as if it were part of the lottery scheme as it was full of red balls. 'Ladies, we'll ask you to come and select a ball from this bowl. It will contain the number of the table you will be heading to first. Please head to your table as soon as you select your ball. No one should sit down until our siren sounds, and then you will have three minutes to get to know the person across from you.' She gave a wave of her hand and lowered her tone just a little. 'I'll remind you all that by attending this cruise, you've agreed to abide by the rules to maintain the dynamic of the love boat's cruise and ensure a safe environment for everyone. No offensive behaviour. You'll treat each other with courtesy, and absolutely no sexual advances.'

Sydney felt her own eyebrows go up. Her brother had actually signed her up for this. He was so dead.

Jen moved back to her fun voice. 'Ladies, come and collect your balls.'

There was such irony in that statement that even Sydney couldn't help but laugh, as did half the room.

She stood for a few seconds watching all the most eager move to the front to select one of the red balls. After a few moments, wondering if she could get away with not moving, a staff member gave her a gracious nudge. 'Madam? Can I assist you?'

Sydney couldn't help but smile as the young steward held out his elbow towards her, and she slipped her hand inside. He escorted to her to the queue, which had moved very quickly. Sydney took a deep breath, internally cursed her brother once more for luck, then swirled her hand around the glass bowl. The number of balls had dwindled since she'd taken her time, but there were still a few. She pulled out her number and glanced at it, forty-six. The tables nearby were numbered in the lower range; hers was nearer the other side of the room. There might still be time for escape.

But the young steward seemed to have the

measure of her. 'Madam.' He gestured with his arm towards the area her table was in. He walked alongside her—as if to ensure she actually got there—glanced at her number again, and had a moment of hesitation when he looked up.

What was it?

The man sitting at her table certainly didn't look like he wanted to be there. It was the one she'd noticed earlier. What a pity. Maybe they could console each other?

But there was something else. The steward gave a low bow of his head. 'Signor Conti,' he murmured as he pulled out the chair for Sydney.

She was momentarily confused. Did the staff know everyone's names? How was that even possible?

She concentrated on the man seated in front of her. Handsome, broad shoulders, clearly Italian, with brooding dark eyes and dark hair. There was no way this guy would struggle to get a date. What on earth was he doing here?

The thought made her a little indignant. She wouldn't struggle to get a date either—difference was, she just didn't want one. Maybe he was the same?

She held out her hand. 'Sydney Scott.'

He blinked, leaving an almost awkward silence. 'Vittorio Conti.'

He seemed familiar. She was sure she didn't know him, but might she have seen him somewhere before?

She gave a loud sigh and raised her drink to him. 'So, did you get conned into this too?'

His brow furrowed. 'Conned?' he said, as if trying to place the word. Her accent did occasionally come off a little strong, so maybe he thought he had misheard her.

'Duped, cheated?'

His forehead flattened and he nodded. 'Ah, conned.' As if he were saying the word entirely differently than her. The edges of his lips hinted upwards. 'Maybe.'

'Now, everyone—' the words cut across them sharply and they both gave a slight jump '—I hope no one has started early.' It was Jen, anxious to keep the room on track. 'So, I'll give you a countdown. Your three minutes start in three, two, one, GO!'

'She's really excited for this.' Sydney smiled as she took a sip of her mai tai.

Something flashed across his eyes. Was it annoyance? 'Maybe it's important to her,' he said carefully.

Sydney was interested. She leaned both elbows on the table and looked at Vittorio. 'Is it important to you?'

* * *

There was the tiniest hint of cleavage in front of him that he was trying not to look at.

He was thinking of a dozen reasons he absolutely shouldn't be here, but this woman in front of him had just started red flags waving in his head—and it wasn't the colour of the dress that had sent him in that direction.

It was the amused smile, and the way she'd just asked the question. Was this woman some kind of journalist looking for a scoop? While he hadn't asked his staff not to identify him, it wouldn't particularly do him any good if it was known the chief executive of the cruise line was taking part in a dating game. He could only imagine how many of his exes might want to comment on that.

He let out an audible groan, and the woman across from him's eyebrows raised. 'Am I that bad?'

Shc was joking, of course she was. Her red dress emphasized her curves and her light tan, and her dark curls were a pleasant change from the poker-straight hair most women seemed to favour these days.

He took a deep breath. 'Not at all,' he said, deciding that for the remaining minutes he might as well play along. 'I am lucky to meet you.'

Her gaze narrowed. It was almost like she

could read his mind. 'When was the last time you did speed dating?' she asked.

'Never,' he admitted.

'Me either. And since we don't know how to do this, how about we do some random, and fun, speed questions?' She gave him a mischievous smile. 'The more bizarre, the better.'

The night was getting stranger and stranger, but a few minutes of silly questions he could do.

He blinked, remembering where he'd seen her—in that strange hat near the check-in desks. It gave him his first question. '*Raiders of the Lost Ark* or *Jurassic Park*?'

'*Raiders.*'

He'd barely finished the question. But her smile was increasing.

'Space, or the bottom of the sea?' she prompted.

'Bottom of the sea,' he replied. 'If I can find Atlantis, that's a bonus.' He held out both hands. 'We're on a ship. You can't possibly expect me to say space.'

She looked amused, and he saw something spark in her eyes. Maybe this wasn't going to be quite as bad as he thought.

'Cannoli or tiramisu?'

She held up both hands. 'Both. Together,' she said firmly.

'No, only one.' He gave her a serious stare.

She blew out a breath. 'Fine. Cannoli.'

It was his turn to look amused. 'Red or white wine?' He was enjoying this and it took him by surprise.

She knew what he wanted her to say. 'Neither, rosé. I'm very particular.'

He wrinkled his nose and pulled back from the table, shaking his head.

She looked him right in the eye. 'Paris or Vienna?' It was a taunt. Leaving out all the magnificent cities of Italy.

'Paris,' he sighed, 'because of the history.' But he played it right back to her. 'Rome or Pompeii?'

She shuddered—she actually shuddered—at the thought of choosing between the two sites.

'One minute!' shouted Jen.

'Rome,' she said, although instantly regretted it. 'Because of the feeling you get when you walk into the Colosseum.'

'Interesting,' he said.

She held up one hand. 'I reserve the right to change that answer at a later date.'

'Tennis or football?' she asked.

'To play, or to watch?'

The counter question kind of caught her off guard it came at her so fast. She shrugged.

'Tennis to play, football to watch,' he responded. He'd leaned a bit closer, and she was getting a better view of those dark eyes. They were brown with a few tiny gold flecks. But what was most annoying was just how perfect his skin was. How did guys manage that? No blemishes. No spots. Just perfect, tanned skin.

'Book or film?' he asked.

She blinked and tore her concentration away from his face. 'That's easy. Always book, but audio book for flights, e-books for train, and a paperback for lying next to the pool.'

'You *are* quite particular, aren't you?'

Sydney mock rolled her eyes. 'You have no idea.'

He leaned forward again, as if he were enjoying this game more than he should. 'If you could time travel, what event would you go back to see?'

She waved a hand. 'Easy. The building of the pyramids.' Then she pulled a face. 'Or the creation of Al-Khazneh.'

He gave her a kind of quizzical glance.

'Petra,' she said, 'The tomb carved out of rock there—the Treasury of the Pharaoh?'

He nodded. 'It's been in films, hasn't it?'

'Yip.'

'So, no wanting to find out the truth about JFK, the moon landing, or the *Titanic*?'

She shook her head. 'I'm not big on conspiracy theories.'

He gave her a careful look. 'Neither am I. I like to believe what I can see.'

Sydney licked her lips, wondering if there was meaning there that she wasn't understanding.

'And we're done!' shouted a delighted Jen. 'Could all gentlemen please leave their tables and come and collect a ball. You'll move to that table for the next three-minute session.'

For a second, neither of them moved. 'We were just getting started.' Sydney smiled as Vittorio stood.

He held out his hand towards her. 'It's been a pleasure, Ms Scott.' The Italian burr did something to the tiny hairs at the back of her neck. She didn't want to be here. She'd hated the mere thought of this. But he'd made it not too bad. In fact, this handsome Italian had made it kind of fun.

She slid her hand into his, letting their skin connect and absolutely ignoring the little sparks running up her arm.

'Signor Conti,' she said, staying in her seat as instructed, and refusing to watch his muscular body walk over to the stage.

Sydney sipped at her mai tai and contemplated ordering another after the next two speed-dating rounds. Two perfectly nice but boring men, who liked to talk about themselves and give her hints at the sort of woman they were looking for.

Needless to say, she didn't fit the bill, and didn't want to.

By the time it was the fourth round, she'd just started sipping a diet soda and wondering how she could get out of here as a familiar figure slid into the seat opposite her.

'What?' She looked around, and then frowned suspiciously at Vittorio. 'What're the odds of you picking this number?'

'Good, when you know the staff,' he said succinctly.

'You work here?' That was it. The kind of vibe she got from him that something wasn't quite correct.

He pulled a face. 'Yes and no.'

He pushed a drink towards her that he'd obviously collected at the bar.

'A mai tai? That's what you're drinking, isn't it?'

She shook her head. 'I'm a lightweight. I've moved onto the diet soda.' She swept her arm outwards. 'Don't want to get tipsy when there's all this talent around. I could ruin my chances.' She could tell that he knew she was being deliberately sarcastic.

He leaned his head on one hand. 'Sydney Scott, what are you really doing here?'

'You tell me yours, and I'll tell you mine,' she responded, letting her eyebrows raise slightly.

'I'm experiencing something close to a nightmare,' he admitted. 'Actually, correct that, I've never had a nightmare that compares with this. For my last two speed dates, one woman told me she wants to get married before she's thirty and to have two children as soon as possible, and the second one wants me to know that she rates all her male *friends*' performances on an online app to share with other women.'

Sydney blinked, then started choking with laughter. 'Really?' She looked around. 'Which ones are they?'

'Stop it,' he hissed, grabbing her arm and pulling her a little towards him so their heads almost met.

She met his brown eyes. 'This wasn't what I meant when I said you tell me yours. But…it's interesting. My two guys were just boring, and self-interested.'

He kept his voice low. 'You don't strike me as the kind of woman that needs a love boat cruise to find a date.'

She feigned wiping her forehead. 'Why, thank you.' He didn't speak again and left her to fill the silence. 'My brother booked this for me. I haven't had a proper holiday for a few years, and he decided in his wisdom he'd book something for me. I knew I was going on a cruise. I didn't know about any of the rest of it.'

Now it was Vittorio's turn to laugh. 'Something tells me that he's in trouble.'

'So much trouble,' she agreed, then gave him a look. 'But that doesn't explain you.'

Vittorio sighed. 'The *Minerva* is our new cruise ship.' He gave her a reluctant look. 'I own the company. I'm the chief executive. I was only here to see the boat off. I was meant to disembark. But—' he took another breath and gave the briefest shake of his head '—because of the flight issues and the eruption at Pompeii, not all the passengers arrived. We were down a significant number of male passengers, and our cruise director, Jen, decided to rope me and another few people in, to even the numbers.'

A wide smile started to spread across Sydney's face. 'This is just your living nightmare, isn't it?'

He nodded. 'Absolutely. But I get the impression it's pretty much your nightmare too.'

'Give me Egypt, dusty sands, digs, and pharaohs any day of the week.'

He tilted his head. 'Those clothes you were wearing when you boarded—that was work? That wasn't some kind of weird cosplay?'

She stared at him for a moment, her brain trying to compute what he'd just said. He'd noticed her when she'd arrived? Interesting. She looked down, even though she was wearing a red dress now, trying to really comprehend this. 'You thought my work gear was cosplay?' she asked incredulously.

Vittorio sat back a little, as if he realised the mistake he'd just made.

Sydney didn't know whether to laugh or cry. This whole thing was just getting more ridiculous by the moment.

'That's why I asked you the Indiana Jones question,' he added, digging himself into an even deeper hole than he was in already.

She shook her head. 'It was a simple shirt and a pair of khaki trousers.'

This time he shook his head. 'No, it was the hat. You definitely had the hat.'

She tightened her face and put her hands on her hips. 'Have you any idea what it's like out there? Ten to fourteen hours a day, searing heat, sand everywhere, fierce winds—'

Vittorio raised his hand. 'Wait. What do you actually do?'

It was like he was trying to slot the pieces of this conversation together.

She threw up her hands. 'I'm an Egyptologist.'

'A what?'

Sydney blew out some air, trying to keep her temper. 'I specialise in ancient Egypt.'

'But what do you actually do?'

'What do you actually do, Mr Chief Executive and I-shouldn't-be-here, I'm-too-good-for-all-this?'

'Whoa.' His voice raised in pitch. 'It's a reasonable question.'

Sydney could sense others turning to look at them. She was sure Jen was currently trying to arrange some alternative activity for the guests, but close by, they were all too busy listening in to Sydney and Vittorio's spat.

'I dig,' she said determinedly. 'I look for past pharaoh tombs, and ancient artefacts that tell the stories of the people who lived there. I've worked on digs in Egypt since I was seventeen.'

He blinked. 'So you're just a female version of Indiana Jones?'

Her face stayed straight, and she delivered a line she'd said one hundred times. 'He stole artefacts and took them back to the US. I don't do that. Artefacts belong in their country of origin.'

Vittorio gave a nod of his head. 'I get that.' Then he gave her a smile. 'But people from the Roman Empire left artefacts all around the world.'

Sydney couldn't resist. 'Some people might call them careless.'

'Ouch!' he said.

'Indiana Jones is make-believe. I'm real, and so is the job that I do.'

He leaned forward, put his head in his hand,

and spoke in a low, deep voice. 'You take this very seriously, don't you?'

She lowered her voice too. 'I do, It's not a job. It's a vocation.'

He gave her a smile. 'Okay, let's make a deal—one that will benefit us both.'

Sydney didn't answer, just let her raised eyebrows do the talking.

Vittorio filled the gap. 'You and I don't really buy into this kind of thing. We know that all the excursions off the ship say that you have to have a date.' He put his hand on his chest. 'I'll be your date. You can explore any archaeological site to your heart's content. If I know the area, I'll show you around. If I don't—' he paused for a second '—I'll get us a private tour. I'm assuming if we say we're a couple, Jen and the rest of the team will leave us alone. We won't need to participate in any more of this.'

'And what do you get out of this?'

He held up his hands. 'I don't get my sexual activities rated on an app and someone doesn't get to rush me into babies and marriage.'

Sydney was instantly suspicious. 'Sounds too good to be true. What else?'

'What do you mean?'

Her eyes swept the large room. 'One of the press people is going to realise who you are. How are you going to do damage control? How will it look for the business if the chief exec joined in on the love boat to get a date?'

He cringed, not even trying to hide the fact he was pulling a face. 'Maybe they'll just think I'm a fun guy?' he said, clearly reaching for the first thing he could think of.

Sydney leaned back in her chair. 'Vittorio Conti, are you known as a fun guy?'

She watched his face, as he clearly wanted to say yes, then contemplated the truth and sighed, rolling his eyes. 'Not always.'

'Not ever?'

He reached over and touched her hand. 'Can't we just think of this as damage control?'

She put her other hand to her chest. 'You mean, I'm your damage control? What if I don't want to be in the press? What if I just want a quiet holiday?'

It was Vittorio's turn to look around the room. 'Do you really want to have to speed date every night with the guys you just met?'

She took a sip of her diet soda. 'Probably not.'

'And if you wanted a quiet holiday, you should probably have given your brother better instructions.'

He was teasing her, and she knew it. The choice was simple. Spend the next thirteen days locked in her executive suite. Or join in all the daily dating activities and find herself a date for every port. Or just agree to hang around with Vittorio, risk a few photographs being taken, but get to see all the sites.

She took another quick look around the room. People were chatting at the bar. A few were still sitting at tables like she was. And more were milling around, looking a bit lost.

She swallowed, then lifted her glass towards him. 'How bad could this be?'

CHAPTER THREE

VITTORIO WONDERED WHAT on earth he had done. He hadn't even taken the time to check the background of the person he'd apparently just signed up to spend time with.

The internet was his friend, and it appeared as though Sydney Scott was exactly who she said she was. Trouble was, the more he read, the more interested and slightly intimidated he became.

He couldn't just have picked someone normal? He shook his head and smiled to himself. Sydney was feisty. She could hold her own. Maybe he should have been a little more open with her.

Vittorio had never been a guy to look for the spotlight for himself. But a few years ago, he thought he'd fallen in love. With a supermodel. Of course. She was beautiful, charming, and addicted to drugs. The latter he'd found out after their engagement.

He'd tried to help her. Tried to get her into programmes. She'd lasted five days at one place and left because her agent had got her another high-paying job. Her mood and temperament were affected. She'd fly off the handle one minute and weep for hours the next.

Work was her saving grace, and when she was working was the only time she seemed to hold things together.

Behind the scenes was an entirely different story. She had frequent outbursts—some documented by the press. As their relationship deteriorated and she didn't want any of the help he offered, she started to give pointed interviews. Implying that Vittorio was controlling, as well as a number of other things.

He'd broken off their engagement and walked away, but not before talking to her agent and agreeing that when she was ready, he was still prepared to help her. He just wasn't about to let false allegations destroy the business he'd been building for years.

There was every chance that once Sydney connected the dots and realised who he was, she would read the internet gossip that was still available and decide she didn't want to spend any time with him whatsoever.

Part of his brain told him that he knew what was out there was all untrue, and completely unfounded. The other part told him to be upfront and honest.

But the truth was, that relationship had damaged him. He had actually loved her. He'd been deeply hurt by her actions. It had made him reluctant to date anyone seriously again. Why open himself up to all that?

He'd never tried a dating app. And had turned down well-meaning friends who tried to pair him off with any of their single acquaintances. It wasn't worth it. It was so much easier to invest all this time and energy into his work. He'd worked twenty-hour days. He'd worked around the clock sometimes to attend international meetings. Some people might call him a control freak, as he struggled to delegate some tasks that he probably should. If he wasn't working, he was at the gym. Sleep and food were essentials that were fitted in when he could. But this?

Being on the cruise ship for the next fortnight, where he couldn't work properly and would be expected to have fake dates and do some sightseeing? It was a stretch. Yes, he did know some Italian sites well. But would he be able to show Sydney around when she'd be looking for in-depth historical or archaeological information? Not a chance.

Just as well sleep was an optional extra. He'd have to spend all his nights doing internet searches on places he'd visited on school trips or with family.

Jen walked into his office, distracting him from his thoughts and putting down an itinerary in front of him. ‘So, first activity is in the theatre, then we have afternoon cocktails in the lounge.’ She glanced at him. ‘We’ve already had some successes. Around forty have declared they are—’ she gave him a smile ‘—coupled up, for the trip into Dubrovnik today.’

‘What about the rest of the passengers?’ It was a fair question. Cruise ships made a percentage of their money on the port day arranged trips.

Jen held up one hand. ‘We’re doing a lucky dip. If people want to go onshore, they just go into a lucky dip and find out who their partner for the day will be just as they disembark.’

Vittorio swallowed, thinking about the other two women he’d met last night. Three minutes had been enough. Five hours, or more, would make him want to hide in his cabin.

‘Let’s get some feedback and see how that goes,’ he said diplomatically.

‘Oh, and count me out. I’ve met someone and going offshore with her.’ He was quick to add that in before Jen told him he was going in the lucky dip too.

‘Who?’

Jen was a typical woman, excellent at multitasking, and had been doing a few other tasks while talking to him. Now he had her full attention.

‘Just someone.’

She lowered her head down next to his. ‘Oh no, you don’t get to do that. Spill.’

He blinked. Jen was always the ultimate professional around him. Now she was talking to him like they were brother and sister, or at the very least good friends. He was still her boss, and he might need to remind her.

So he didn’t say a word, merely raised his eyebrows.

She put her hand on her chest. ‘What? I was expecting you to be available to join in the activities today. The photographers and a few online streamers had expressed interest in maybe getting a few snaps with you. If you’re about to spoil things, I’m only asking in case it will help with the publicity for the ship.’

He took a breath. ‘It’s the woman from the foyer yesterday. Sydney Scott. I met her at the speed dating last night, and she seems…nice.’

He knew better than to tell Jen they were both trying to get out of the love boat antics.

‘Nice?’ Jen stood up, looking instantly suspicious. ‘Who is she?’

He waved a hand. ‘She’s an archaeologist, no, an Egyptologist. Smart lady. Spends most of her time doing digs in Egypt.’ He pulled a face. ‘She’s the real deal, and I didn’t really help things when I asked if she was cosplaying Indiana Jones when she came on board.’

Jen's mouth fell open, then, after a few seconds, she started to laugh. 'Tell me that you didn't.'

'Oh, I did,' he admitted. 'It didn't go down well.'

'I'll bet it didn't.' She was still laughing.

'What?' he said. 'I absolutely wasn't seeing things yesterday. Someone was definitely dressed up as Princess Leia.'

Jen nodded, still laughing to herself. 'Someone definitely was. And we had a few others who I think were doing Carrie from *Sex and the City.*'

'Who?' He had no idea what she was talking about.

'Never mind. Another show.'

But Jen was still shaking her head. 'So, Sydney Scott, we moved her to the executive suites. She didn't look too happy about being here.' Her eyes shot to Vittorio's, full of suspicion. 'Is there anything I should know?'

'No,' he said in too breezily a manner, which just made Jen narrow her eyes further.

'You're going onshore, in Dubrovnik?'

He nodded. She folded her arms. 'What are you going to do?'

'Haven't decided yet.'

'You haven't booked on to one of the tours?'

He shook his head, then looked Jen in the eye. 'We're looking for something a little more…

romantic.' The smile spread across his face as he said the word. He was daring her to challenge him.

She drew her eyes up and down his body. 'Do you know the temperature in Dubrovnik? I suggest you go down to the shops and find something more suitable to wear.'

He looked down at his suit trousers and pale blue long-sleeved shirt. She might have a point.

But Jen wasn't finished. 'Something more romantic, you say?'

He didn't respond, not wanting to get into a question-and-answer session that she would so clearly win. She stood in silence for a few moments and then spun and headed to the door. 'Well, good luck with that. I'll tip the photographer off.'

Sydney had eaten breakfast alone. It had been almost…majestic. Javier had brought her exactly what she'd asked for, toasted white bread, salted butter, tomato, and a poached egg, along with a fancy smoothie she hadn't asked for, in an interesting shade of green. It had tasted amazing. And she'd enjoyed her breakfast while sitting in the most comfortable robe in the world, listening to an audio book and looking out at the ocean. Why had she never considered a cruise before?

She'd finished breakfast by sipping some

lemon and ginger tea before dressing in some cool clothing—a pair of knee-length beige shorts and a loose coral-coloured top—with a swimsuit underneath—and a pair of trainers for any walking they might be doing. Her bag had her sunscreen and sunglasses, and she held her large floppy hat in her hand as she made her way to the area to disembark. She'd arranged to meet Vittorio here last night and was surprised at how her stomach was currently churning. This was nothing. This was casual. A pleasant way for them to pass the time with no pressure.

Except there was. What if after a day in her company, he decided he didn't like her, and she fell into the same category as the other two women he'd met last night?

Well, she didn't plan on getting up close and personal and rating him on an app, nor did she plan to try to convince him to marry her—so at least she had that going for her.

She tried to reassure herself that equally, Vittorio could turn out be the same as the boring men she'd met last night. But somehow, she knew that was unlikely to be the case.

There was something about him last night. He met all the criteria for the handsome, well-built Italian. The hair, the eyes, the physique, and the accent. If you'd asked Sydney previously, she would have said she would never fall for such a cliché.

But something about Vittorio was intriguing. It could just be that they were both in the wrong place at the wrong time. But they both recognised the humour in the situation. It was almost like they were giving each other permission to have fun with it. She'd told him she didn't really do holidays, and she got the impression that he was very similar, so would it really be a bad thing to have a few fun days together?

The idea danced around in her head. She didn't do flings. Or, at least, she never had before. But then again, her dating history was a disaster. Maybe it was time to throw all the previous rules out the window and find some new ones? Sydney could feel heat rush into her cheeks. This was ridiculous. Although she was sure he'd glimpsed down her cleavage last night, she didn't have a single clue if he found her attractive. Sure, it seemed like there had been a little spark between them, but that could've all been in her imagination. Last thing she needed alongside the love boat trauma was some extra humiliation at being rejected. She pushed the romantic thoughts aside.

Her thoughts drifted back to some of the things her brother had said. She knew he was worried about her. It wasn't exactly a secret that she'd taken the death of their mother hard. She'd let him organise the funeral, attended, wept volumes, and then scurried back to Egypt as quickly as she could. Work was where she could focus. She didn't want to think about the house that needed to be emptied and sold—the house that held a million happy memories for her. Running from her feelings was what Sydney did best. She'd learned it through her disastrous relationships and continued it following the loss of her mother. Avoidance seemed so much easier than actually sitting down and feeling the pain. She wasn't sure when she would ever be ready for that.

She pushed all those thoughts aside and as she walked down the steps, she was pleasantly surprised to see him waiting and scanning the crowd for her.

He had on a pair of dark navy shorts and a white polo shirt, and a baseball hat in hand. He gave her a smile then held up one hand. '*Game of Thrones* fan?'

She shook her head, wondering what on earth he was talking about. 'Never seen an episode—haven't had time. But I've heard good things, so I'll catch up at some point.'

He nodded. 'Then it's swimming in the blue caves or visiting the Kravica waterfalls.'

She contemplated for a second. The *Jaws*

theme tune sounded again. 'Waterfalls sound good.'

'Do you travel okay? We'll be in the car for about two hours.'

She nodded. 'As long as we stop somewhere for a coffee, that's fine.'

'And do you have your passport?'

She pulled it from her bag.

'Perfect, then let's go.'

They filed out, scanning their cards at the gangplank to confirm they'd left the ship, then he led her down the long port walkway. There were a number of coaches waiting, but he took her to a limo.

The driver was waiting and opened the door for them. The cool air conditioning was apparent straight away.

'Why did you ask me about *Game of Thrones*?' she asked as the car started.

'A lot of the scenes in the series were filmed in and around Dubrovnik,' he said. 'Some people come here purely for the tour of where the scenes were shot.'

She gave him a half smile. 'You mean fans that might cosplay?'

He groaned. 'You're not going to let that go, are you?'

'Not a chance.' She smiled as she sank back into the comfortable leather seats.

The countryside flew past, with the driver answering any questions she had, and the transfer between Croatia and Bosnia was smooth.

'It's just up here,' said the driver, gesturing ahead as Sydney practically had her nose pressed to the glass.

Everywhere was green. Mountains, trees, and a lush landscape that seemed to just roll out in front of them. As they turned into the entrance to the falls, Sydney caught her breath.

It was beautiful. She hardly waited for the car to stop before she opened the door and stepped out.

'Have you been here before?' she asked Vittorio over her shoulder.

'Never,' he said, stepping alongside her to admire the view.

Vittorio gestured for her to walk through the ticket office, where he already had tickets. They moved along a paved path with stairs. As they strolled downwards it didn't take long for the full beauty of the falls to come into sight.

From where they were positioned, it was like a giant secret spot. The waterfalls were so surrounded by trees that it almost looked like the water was pouring from them. The falls were curved, around twenty-five metres tall, but broad, with at least twenty cascading waterfalls into the emerald green lake beneath.

'It's like something from a kid's fairy book,' she said as they moved closer.

There were other people around. A few boats kayaking on the water, other people swimming, and a few families at the water's edge. The air around them was hot.

As they moved towards the edge of the lake, Sydney couldn't help but reach down and touch the water.

'Oooh,' she said quickly, then laughed. 'It's colder than I thought.'

'Are you up for a swim?'

There were a number of other people braving the cold waters. Sydney put her hand on her hips for a moment to contemplate things. 'There are no crocodiles in Bosnia, are there?'

He gave her a surprised look.

'I live in Egypt most of the year. Crocodiles in the Nile are common. Now, there's a river I wouldn't set foot in.'

She kept glancing around, taking in the view, then jumped as his voice came just behind her.

'It's a fairy-tale amphitheatre of water, rock, and greenery,' he mused.

She turned towards him, smiling. 'Are you a poet?'

He frowned and shook his head. 'Not at all.'

'Well, that was almost poetic.'

He held out one arm. 'I'm just appreciating the beauty of the place.'

She glanced at his clothes. 'Did you bring your swimming gear?'

He nodded. 'Do you have a costume under there?'

Sydney pulled the coral strap of her swimsuit and pinged it. 'Always ready.' She looked around again. 'You know, this is the first time since I started this cruise that I haven't heard the *Jaws* theme tune when I've looked at water.'

He gave her an amused smile. 'You don't like the ocean?'

'I don't like what's *in* the ocean,' she corrected.

'It's a big place. And sharks don't generally bother with humans.'

'I know the theory,' she agreed. 'But I've watched the films.' She tapped the side of her head. 'My brother made me watch all the scary films as kids and they've implanted in my brain. So, it doesn't matter what perfectly reasonable argument you have—I look at the sea, ocean, anything that reaches the horizon, and I automatically hear the tune.'

He nudged her. 'So an enclosed lake isn't so bad.'

She waved her hand from side to side. 'I can do the more reasonable thinking about a lake.

Particularly when I can see the edges, and the waterfalls, and anything that comes over them.'

He laughed and pointed in a direction of the café at the water's edge. 'How about some refreshments before we swim? Maybe the water will heat a little as the day goes on.'

'You did cheat me out of a coffee earlier,' she joked as they started to walk in that direction.

'Hey, I asked you, but you said you didn't want to stop.'

She shrugged. 'True, but I'll let you buy me cake now too.'

This was easier than she'd thought. He'd been a little quiet on the drive here, taking a few work calls, then apologising for that, and asking if she minded if he answered a few emails.

But this wasn't a date. They were both using their own thoughts on the love boat concept to their advantage. So, she couldn't claim to be offended or hurt. But even though she'd been distracted by her audiobook, she'd still been watching Vittorio with interest.

His Italian voice was hypnotic. And he was expressive. He used his hands when he spoke, meaning his phone had ended up wedged between his ear and his neck, and she'd wanted to laugh at him.

But the calls and emails had been over quickly, and they'd both spent the rest of the journey asking the driver occasional questions about their surroundings.

She looked back at the glistening lake, then back to Vittorio, who had joined the queue for coffee and was gesturing for her to come over. This day wasn't shaping up too badly.

She noticed him getting a few second glances. So, it wasn't only her that thought he was handsome. The thought of a fling had dissipated on the drive here. Surely if he'd been the least bit interested in her, he'd have left the work behind and paid more attention to her in the limo? She was a bit embarrassed now about those thoughts that had clearly been one-sided. But this was a beautiful place she'd never visited before, and Vittorio was a hospitable enough host. It would just have to be enough.

Vittorio watched as Sydney surveyed the people around them before finally moving over and spotting the cakes in the glass counter.

He'd been jittery in the car. Once he'd remembered he hadn't dated properly in four years, conversation had kind of died in his throat. It was ridiculous. He'd never struggled to talk to a woman before, but Sydney, with all her qualifications in a vastly different area that he knew nothing about, was kind of intimidating.

He'd used the work excuse for a bit, but Sydney had seemed unperturbed and listened to something in her headphones, before leaning forward and asking the driver some questions.

Vittorio's stomach had squeezed. Was that nerves? Because he really didn't recognise the feeling. It was amazing how being around an attractive woman he wanted to impress could turn him into a teenager all over again.

He gave himself a shake. He was supposed to be showing her around and treating her to all the sites.

'What kind of coffee do you like?' he asked, trying to get things back on track.

'Skinny latte.'

'And what kind of cake do you want?'

She waited a few moments before finally pointing to one adorned with strawberries and fresh cream. 'That one, please.'

He ordered, then she moved over to a table next to the lake as he carried the tray over.

She looked at his cake and sighed. 'The chocolate one, I looked at that too.'

'Are you sure you're not Italian?' he asked as he slid their coffees and cakes from the tray.

'What do you mean?'

He lifted a knife. 'Because if there isn't a lemon cake available, we'll always pick chocolate. Do you want to split?'

She frowned. 'What do you mean?'

'Just about every Italian woman I know does that. Picks a cake, then always wishes they'd chosen yours. So, usually we split, and have half each.'

'You take a lot of Italian women for cake?'

'I'm thirty-five, I've taken a few women for cake,' he said easily, although he knew that wasn't really what she was asking, and considering how strangely nervous he'd felt earlier, he was trying to appear much more suave than he was actually feeling.

She gave a slow nod. 'Yes, I want to split.' She lifted one hand and grinned. 'But you know the rules about splitting, don't you?'

He gave her an amused glance. 'No, what are the rules?'

She grinned. 'Well, you're cutting, so I get to choose which half I want. Of both.'

He still had the knife poised in his hand. 'Stakes are high. Better make sure I make this an even split.'

He cut the chocolate cake and then the strawberry one, then waited while she chose her halves and slid them onto the plates. He was starting to relax a little more now. Sydney Scott was extraordinarily easy to be around.

'If you hadn't already mentioned a brother, I would definitely have pegged you as having one after that move.'

Sydney licked her finger, which had got a little chocolate on it. 'Applies to any sibling really. Didn't you feel cheated as an only child?'

He shook his head. 'I'm from a big Italian family. I have lots of cousins, so I never really felt like an only child.' Then he held up one finger. 'But not a word about the mafia, or *The Godfather*. My family is entirely normal.'

She laughed as she took a sip of her coffee. 'Bit like when I tell someone I'm an archaeologist and they ask Indiana Jones questions.'

'Touche,' he replied, cringing internally. 'You're not going to let me forget about that, are you?'

She winked. 'I'll stop if you put a horse head on my bed.'

He let his head sag onto his forearms at the *Godfather* reference. 'Is this going to stop at any point?'

She shook her head. 'Probably not, so just take it like a man.'

He shook his head. 'So, tell me about your job. Why did you go into that area?'

She rolled her eyes. 'Would you believe I watched a film as a six-year-old and it sparked my interest?'

'Raiders?'

'Nope, *Antony and Cleopatra*.'

'Weren't you a bit young for that at six?'

'Absolutely, but it was a Saturday afternoon, and that's what was on the TV that day. I watched it from start to finish. Got books from the library about Egypt. Read everything I could. Women in history are fascinating, you know. Cleopatra was a woman before her time. She should be even more famous than she actually is, and it kind of annoys me that some people only think of her in the context of Mark Antony.' She leaned forward and whispered, 'Because some people would say he was actually a bit of a dick.' She smiled. 'But anyway, I discovered I loved history and the ancient world. I learned about Stonehenge, Pompeii, Petra, and Machu Picchu. Spent a long time immersed in the Colosseum and Pantheon. Italy can be quite interesting.' There was a spark of mischief in her eyes.

'Thank goodness,' he said. 'I'd hate to disappoint.'

He gave her a measured look. 'So, have you been everywhere you wanted to go?'

'Not a chance.' She took a bite of cake. 'I had plans to go to China and see the Terracotta Army but—' she shrugged '—Covid, and I've never been able to reschedule. It's still on my list, along with a whole host of other places.'

'Do you live in Egypt all year round?'

She nodded. 'Mainly. I still have a place in England.' Her voice faded a little, and he watched her swallow and catch her thoughts before she continued. 'I work on digs for around eight months of the year. Then, I help catalogue everything for the Museum of Antiquities, plus some of their backlog. I do occasional lectures—mainly online, for my old university. Time off is…' She searched for the right word. 'Fleeting.' She smiled.

'You don't sound sorry.'

'I'm not. I love what I do. Not many people can say that about their job.' She gave him a careful look. 'What about you? You seem kind of young for a chief executive.'

He lifted his shoulders in a half shrug. 'Maybe I am. But I did a joint business and engineering degree and did a placement with the cruise company when I was still a student. They offered me a full-time job once I completed my degree, and I was lucky enough to work in different parts of the organisation. Our family had some money, which I chose to invest, leading me to be a major shareholder. In the past seven years, we've launched four new ships, and business is doing well. I trust my staff. They do a good job and take pride in their work.'

'What about the downsides of cruising?'

'Which are?' He could feel all his defences automatically falling into place.

'The chance of disease, pirates, issues with the ports or some of the crew.'

He straightened in his chair, a little surprised at her knowledge for an area she said she knew little about. He took a forkful of chocolate cake before he answered.

'We're lucky in the Med that pirates are rarely an issue, but all captains know exactly what to do in situations like those, and communication amongst us, other cruise lines, and port authorities makes sure any chance of an incident is low. We've never had an incident on board any of our cruise liners.'

She nodded. 'And the rest?' she asked as she sipped her coffee.

'Norovirus—the dreaded disease that spreads quickly on cruise liners—is always a possibility. We have protocols we follow at the first sign of anyone being unwell—usually it's just an issue of a sensitive stomach for someone who's eaten something on a shore excursion that hasn't agreed with them. As for our crew? We pay the best rates in the Med for our lower-ranking crew. A lot of them are supporting families back home and I appreciate that. We also have the most spacious crew quarters, and that can make a big difference for people. And while crew work can be seasonal, a number of our staff work with us year after year—so we must be doing something right.'

She sat back in her chair and looked at him, her dark curls catching in the breeze that was coming off the lake. The air was warm, and the heat was building around them. Sydney Scott was an impressive lady. The fact that her blue eyes were questioning but steady intrigued him. It looked like there were another hundred questions waiting for him.

'Tell me about your family,' he said, and noticed immediately the flash across those eyes.

'You already know about my brother, Pete.'

'Well, I know he booked you a holiday you didn't really agree to. Why?'

She pressed her lips together for a second, and he knew he was going to get only what she wanted to tell him.

'He knows how hard I work, and apparently conspired with my boss to make me take some holidays.'

'Is that a bad thing?'

She tucked some hair behind her ear. 'Yes and no.' She gave a small sigh. 'I don't have the best history with dating, and this whole love boat thing is probably his idea of a joke.' Her gaze met his. 'But I've assured him I will kill him when I get back, him and his wife.'

'What's she like?'

'Jess? Nice, a good match for Pete. They met at university and got married when they both landed their first jobs. She's a teacher and he's in accounts.' She paused for a moment. 'They've been trying for a family for a while and it hasn't worked out yet. I'm hoping it does, they'd be good parents.'

'And would you be a good aunt?'

Her eyes widened as if she was surprised by the question. 'Me? I would be the best aunt.'

He leaned his head on one hand lazily. 'You would be the fun auntie, wouldn't you? Feed them all the things they aren't allowed, get them hyper, do all the fun stuff, and then take them home.'

Instead of being offended she nodded. 'Isn't that what an auntie's job is?'

He smiled and stood up to clear their plates and cups. 'Ready enough to brave the water?'

Sydney stood and put her hands on her hips for a second, staring at the green water. 'There could be a Loch Ness Monster in there, couldn't there? A lake, a loch, they're the same thing.'

'Would you prefer a swimming pool?' he asked with amusement.

She waved a hand. 'Oh, swimming pools are fine. I can see the bottom. I can see what's in there.'

He looked out at the lake. 'All that's in there

is a bunch of rocks and some cold water. We'll be fine. Come on.'

He watched her take a breath. He could see the determined look in her eye, the one that stubbornly wouldn't submit to her fear.

'Scared a shark will jump over the falls?' he teased.

He watched her ponder whether that was at all a possibility and then dismiss the idea, with a quick scowl at him.

She yanked some suntan spray from her bag and rubbed it into her skin. 'Let's go.'

It only took them a moment to shed their outer layers. Swimming costumes didn't hide much, but Vittorio wouldn't let his eyes linger on her curves. It would be impolite.

Then again, the coral costume looked as if it had been designed to show off the swell of her breasts, her defined arms, the incline of her waist, and the further curves of her hips. It was clear she was fit. The physicality involved in the digs was apparent in the muscle structure of her arms and shoulders.

'Ouch.' She pulled her foot back after her toes hit the cold water. Now she was smiling in shock and gave a theatrical shudder. 'Are you sure about this?'

Her skin visibly prickled next to him, and he knew straight away not to hang around.

Vittorio braced himself and waded in, his breath catching at the base of his throat as his body responded to the temperature. He was laughing as he continued out to his chest, then turned around to face her. 'What? It's warm in here.'

He kept moving in an attempt to let his body get used to the temperature.

She wasn't fooled at all, but accepted the challenge, taking a breath and wading out next to him, but keeping her arms firmly across her chest until her shoulders were beneath the water.

'Whose idea was this?' she challenged.

'Everyone says we'll love it after,' he conceded, 'But keep moving until we've fooled our bodies into enjoying it.'

She nodded to a family drifting past on kayaks. 'I think they had the right idea.'

'Too late now,' he agreed. He pointed to rocks at the far side of the lake. 'Are you okay swimming? Will you make it over there?'

He suddenly realised he hadn't even asked her if she could swim and felt a wave of momentary panic.

But Sydney looked at him with a gleam in her eye. 'Race you,' she said, before putting her head in the water with her moving arms in a fast crawl.

It took him a second to react, and when he

did, she was already a good part in front of him. With his longer limbs and stroke, it didn't take him long to catch up, and he touched the rocks just in front of her. This was a woman who'd clearly spent her life racing against her brother.

'Spoil sport,' she proclaimed, slightly breathless, her cheeks with a hint of pink and her curly hair sleeked back from her face.

Now he could see the freckles across the bridge of her nose, and the light suntan on her skin.

'Happy to race you back,' he said, but she shook her head.

'Let's cross the lake and sunbathe a little at the other side, it looks a little quieter,' she said. 'And my body is now thinking that the temperature in here is entirely normal.' She pointed to some other people at the side of the lake, testing the temperature for the first time and all running back shrieking.

'Amateurs,' he joked.

She moved in front of him, this time with easy strokes, crossing the lake in a matter of minutes before wading out of the water and finding a spot at the side of the lake just near one of the waterfalls.

He climbed out next to her and lay down, nodding over to the area near the café. 'If only we'd planned this better and brought our things with us.'

She shook her head, sending a scattering of water drops over his chest.

'Hey!'

She laughed. 'I can still see our bags. They're fine. Don't be such a worry wart.'

'A what?'

He leaned on one elbow towards her and noticed that she'd frozen for a second.

For a few moments, there was nothing. Then, a noise like she was clearing her throat, something between a cough and a choke. She shook her head again, but this time more subdued said, 'A worry wart,' her voice quiet, almost inaudible next to the background crash of the waterfalls.

'What does that mean?'

She licked her lips, then looked up at him. 'It's just a saying, from back home.' She gave a small smile. 'Someone I know used to say it. It means worrying about nothing really.'

He got that feeling again, of half a story. Of something left unsaid. Vittorio wasn't the type of person to push. He'd never do that. If she wanted to tell him something, she would.

He gave a nod of his head. 'Who wants a pair of beach towels, anyhow?'

He sensed there was so much more to Sydney Scott than she'd revealed. She had such a different personality from his previous partner, Alona. True, Alona had also worried about her career, but the world of a supermodel was entirely different from Sydney's job. Alona could have a meltdown over a blemish, a graze on her thigh, or a hint of sun on her skin. She'd really been a party girl, and while that had been fun for a few months, it wasn't a lifestyle he'd really aspired to. When things had started to disintegrate between them, and the initial buzz of attraction had faded, he'd felt quite sorry for her, but Alona would have hated that if she'd known.

Sydney mused for a second. 'Beach towels,' she said with a hint of pining in her voice, then gave him a smile and leaned back, letting the sun warm her face. 'Let's give it half an hour. You have sunscreen on, don't you?'

He nodded.

'Good, we'll dry off, and then go back in and do it all again.'

He put his hands behind his head and rested back. Sydney closed her eyes, and within a few minutes she looked as if she were sleeping.

Vittorio wasn't quite sure what to make of her. She was bright, intelligent, and he only knew a tiny part of her. Maybe this hadn't been such a bad idea?

Getting to know Sydney Scott might be more fun than he'd given her credit for. Sure, he'd been upfront about not really wanting to be involved in the whole love boat scenario, but that didn't mean he couldn't use the rest of their time to his advantage.

It had been a while since he'd been around a woman like Sydney. In fact, he couldn't actually remember ever being around a woman like Sydney.

He'd dated some of his cousins' friends, a girl in his course at university, a few women from his local city, and then Alona. Parts of him were stirring. Four years was a long time not to date.

He gave a quiet smile at the random facts she'd just thrown at him about cruise ships. Had she done some internet searching herself, so she could try to impress him? He liked the thought of it, but wouldn't want to place a bet.

It could be that Sydney Scott just knew a bit of something about everything. He did have a few friends like that.

He was glad she'd been unlucky the other night and met two men that had bored her. She was beautiful, and he was quite sure that the hundreds of other men on board wouldn't all be boring. There was a chance that she could actually meet someone that she'd like. Was he being selfish here? Asking her to play along with this idea to keep people at bay?

It seemed like they both had bad dating histories, and he did wonder what kind of fools had walked away from a woman like Sydney.

But how could he live up to his part of the equation here?

He'd promised to show her some of the best archaeological sites in the Med. Would she object if that also included a little flirting? On a ship that had been deemed the love boat, it would seem almost unprofessional to not include some flirting in their interactions.

It was time for him to live up to his promises.

Vittorio Conti had some learning to do.

CHAPTER FOUR

SYDNEY WAS DEFINITELY CONFUSED. She'd come on holiday expecting to lie next to a pool and forget about the world. She'd then been sideswiped by the cruise ship, and even more so by the love boat scenario.

She still wasn't on board for it. But Vittorio Conti was…interesting.

Things weren't helped by the fact he was devastatingly handsome. The accent sent little shivers down her spine, but she was slightly suspicious of how colloquial some of his speech was. Had he spent time in the UK at some point?

She was curious as to what being chief executive of a cruise ship company actually meant. He'd asked a lot of questions around her job, and she hadn't really had much chance to return the favour.

She was embarrassed to say she'd napped on the way back to the cruise ship. She'd intended to ask if they could have a look around Dubrovnik before they boarded again, but by the time she'd opened her eyes, the chance was gone.

When they'd reboarded he'd excused himself, and Sydney had gone back to her room to freshen up, then taken a walk to explore the cruise ship a bit more.

She was browsing the exclusive shops on board when someone approached her. 'Hey, would you mind answering a few questions for us?'

Sydney was confused. 'About what?'

The young man smiled enthusiastically. 'It's just about your customer experience. This is our first time doing a love boat cruise, and we want to make sure all our customers are happy.'

'Okay,' she agreed, leaning in next to him to view the questions on the screen.

'We'll start with the basics, your name, your job, and your age.'

She took a breath. 'I'm Sydney Scott, I'm twenty-nine, and I'm an Egyptologist.'

She saw the eyes widening, and wondered if she should have given a different job description. She could have said she worked in a museum, though that wasn't strictly true. That might have made her sound a little more regular.

The guy nudged her. 'So, it isn't part of the questions, but tell me more.'

She smiled and gave more or less the same response she'd given Vittorio last night. 'I studied archaeology at university, then specialised in Egyptology. I've been on a large number of digs in Egypt and have then catalogued countless artefacts that have been found. I supervise students and occasionally lecture at universities.'

The guy nodded enthusiastically but then pulled a face. 'I've got to go back to the questions now, sorry. So, what brings you to a cruise ship that is destined for love?'

'My brother booked this for me. I had no idea until I boarded.'

This made him laugh and exchange a look with the camera man. 'And how do you feel about that?'

She gave a tight smile. 'My brother will be dealt with.'

He glanced back at his tablet. 'So, what are you looking for in a man?'

It was an interesting question. 'I'm not really sure I'm looking for a man.'

She realised that might have come out wrong. 'I love my work. It keeps me so busy, I'm not sure I have time for a relationship right now.'

'But if you did have time, what would you want?'

She took a moment. What did she want? She wasn't sure she'd ever really asked herself the question.

'Someone who can give me space to do my

work. Someone who is interesting, someone I can talk to. And trust, trust is a big issue for me.'

'So, is there anyone on the boat that's sparked your interest?'

Sydney felt a little heat rush into her cheeks. She wasn't sure if she'd been targeted here. No one had really connected her to Vittorio, and she didn't want to give their deal away.

'I've met a few interesting people,' she said noncommittally. It seemed like the easiest answer to give, with no specifics.

'Still open to looking for love?' the guy prompted again.

Sydney swallowed. 'I'm open to enjoying the rest of the cruise,' she said.

He asked a few more generic questions about what she thought about the facilities on the ship, and if she was happy with the safety rules that were in place for all participants on the love boat.

'Okay, thanks,' he said, fixing a smile on his face, 'I appreciate your time.'

'Need to do a little shopping.' She gave a nod and made her way over to the shops before he could ask her anything else.

Her heart was beating quicker in her chest. Had she just embarrassed herself?

She was trying to remember everything she'd said. Maybe she shouldn't have told them her real job. What if she became ridiculed online? A laughing stock of the university?

Panic threatened to rush through her. She walked into the first shop and started blindly looking through the rails. Distraction was absolutely what she needed right now. She definitely didn't want to think about Vittorio. Their agreement was more or less some kind of business deal, convenient for them both without any commitment or complexity.

She likely shouldn't have agreed to exploring onshore locations together. He was only doing it as a courtesy.

But she couldn't help but admire his physique yesterday. He didn't wear a ring. Had not mentioned another half. Indeed, he surely wouldn't have agreed to take part in the love boat shenanigans if he was committed somewhere else.

Then again, Sydney had seen a few episodes of reality TV. Not everyone was what they claimed to be. She would just ask him directly when they next met up.

But when would that be? The next port was Santorini, and there was a whole host of archaeological sites that could be explored. She hadn't made any solid arrangements with him yet. There was always a chance that maybe he'd changed his mind.

It was ridiculous to even think about him in

those terms. But then her hand touched a dress in the store she was in. Silver. Something she would never normally go for. It was too glamourous. Just not her at all.

'Would you like to try it on?' asked the assistant, appearing at her side.

'No,' said Sydney distractedly. 'It's beautiful, but not really what I would wear.'

'Why don't you try it on? Even if it's only for a moment. I think it would suit you.' The assistant had lowered her voice and was talking to Sydney in a conspiratorial manner, as if she were her friend.

The long dress with tiny spaghetti straps was gorgeous. The material caught the light no matter which way it was held. It was like something one would wear in a film studio rather than real life.

She gave a little sigh. 'Oh, okay then.'

The assistant swept her into a dressing room, and moments later she was looking at her reflection in a full-length mirror.

'Wow,' she said, as the assistant stepped behind her and held up her curls.

'It would look spectacular with your hair up. Our salon could do that for you.'

For a moment, Sydney was caught. This was so far away from her real life—from the baggy shirts, practical trousers, and mountains of sand that caught in the creases of her skin.

She wished she was in one of the many movies where a woman got a temporary makeover—but she knew how they all turned out and that it was entirely silly.

Sydney Scott was far too old for silly dreams.

She'd heard other people talking about the on-board shops. How they were exclusive, and very expensive. How even the most practical things—like toothpaste—cost much more than they should. One man had even joked that he'd have to remortgage his house to buy a watch that he'd seen on board. What was she actually doing in here?

'It's beautiful,' she said. 'Thank you for letting me try it. Let me think about it.'

It seemed the best way to put the sales assistant off. Sydney wasn't sure if they worked on some kind of commission, and she'd hate to think she'd wasted the girl's time. Then again, she hadn't even looked at the price tag of the dress. That might kill every other thought dead.

But whether she worked on commission or not, the sales assistant waved her hand. 'No problem, but give me your name so if you change your mind, you can just call and I'll put the dress aside for you.'

'Sydney Scott,' she said, wondering if she

would check her online tab later and find the dress charged to her account. Would that be a bad thing? But where on earth in her real life could she actually go in a dress like that?

Just then, another customer walked into the store, so Sydney waved and ducked out the door before anything else caught her eye.

'What do you mean "up the stakes"?' asked Vittorio.

'To help with the publicity. They want to identify a few couples that have already been paired and photograph them on a few occasions, rather than just snapping random people all the time,' Jen replied.

'I thought they dealt with all these things in the editing for the publicity? Don't they photograph everyone to begin with, and then just use the footage they need as things progress?'

'In an ideal world—yes. But some of our content is being livestreamed, which complicates things. Plus, they only have one real photography crew. On other programmes, they start with multiple crews to capture everyone. The crew here don't really have the time for that.'

'I understand the logic, but why do I get the feeling I won't like where this goes next?'

She gave him her most winning smile. 'They

suggested you might like to be part of one of the couples.'

'What? No!' The reaction was instantaneous.

Jen held up her hands. 'Before you make a snap decision, I suggest you look at this.'

She handed him her tablet and he watched an advert that was playing on the most popular video channel. The advert was for the love boat *Minerva*.

There was catchy music playing to snapshots of guests arriving, some looking excited, some looking pensive. There was a one second glimpse of Sydney arriving and catching sight of the love boat sign. She looked horrified, and you could see the realisation washing over her. It was actually a perfect moment. A wide shot of the welcome drinks, followed by the speed-dating event in the ballroom. Then the moment he might have dreaded had he known it existed. Vittorio, in his dark suit, with an equally dark look in his eyes while sitting in the ballroom. The caption next to him was *Is everyone really looking for love?* In the blink of an eye, it cut to couples clearly flirting with each other. A hand on an arm. Another arm slipping around a waist, and things finished with the phrase *Will the* Minerva *lead to lasting love?*

'That has to come down,' he said immediately.

'Really?' asked Jen, then she pointed to the

numbers beneath the video. It had already hit one million, and as he watched it was rapidly rising.

He groaned. 'Why do people like this stuff?'

'Because it's new, exciting. People imagine themselves being on this boat and having this experience. This is exactly the kind of publicity and attention we were trying to gather.' She looked extremely pleased with herself. 'Ask me about enquiries.'

He didn't get a chance to respond because a graph with an almost vertical trend line appeared in front of him. It showed the number of potential customers who'd enquired about booking on a cruise similar to that of the *Minerva*.

'But we don't have any other cruises like this. The *Minerva* cruise is a one-off,' he said quickly, his brain going to the place she clearly wanted it to.

Jen corrected him. 'This was a "wait and see how it goes" situation. You have a meeting this morning to determine if you are going to amend some cruises to have the same events. It looks like bookings for that could be off the charts.' She was grinning broadly.

Vittorio sat back in his chair. 'I don't get it. There's only one photography crew. How on earth will they capture what they want?'

His brain was still buzzing with how they

could juggle this, in amongst their normal cruise ship schedules.

Jen lowered her gaze for a second. 'Well, our ship crew is helping them out.'

'What?' Vittorio's head whipped up from the screen to her.

She pulled a face. 'They've been encouraged to capture any nice, or dramatic, moments. To let the photography crew know of any possible pairings. There's a central database for them to upload any footage.'

Vittorio stood up, 'That sounds intrusive. I don't want our crew distracted by all this. I want them to do their job.'

'And they *are* doing their job,' assured Jen. 'This was all checked by Legal. People knew what they were signing up for when agreeing to come on this cruise. And this just helps the photographers keep on top of everything.' She glanced up at the door of the office. There were a number of people milling past. 'If you want, we could think of onboarding more crew at the next port.'

He gave a slow nod as he checked some of the comments beneath the video, then checked some social media feeds. 'The initial publicity is looking good. This could, potentially, make the cruise line soar.'

Vittorio was trying to weigh all this in his

head. Of course, he wanted the cruise ship company to do well. If they changed the itineraries of a few ships and bookings went up, everyone would be happy. But there was a chance this was all a flash in the pan. Something that wouldn't last.

Cruise ship holidays were a staple for some people. They came back year after year because they liked the changing itineraries, the fact they stopped in a different port every day, and that they had everything at their fingertips.

Singles didn't really come on cruise ship holidays, and if they did, it would be a whole different dynamic.

'I'm not sure about all this,' he said warily. 'There's so much to think about.'

'There is,' Jen agreed, 'but in the meantime, this is still the maiden voyage of the *Minerva* and we want it to continue to be a success. We want people talking about the ship, and the facilities on board. We want them talking about how great the crew are, how great the food is, and how accessible everything is.'

'We do,' agreed Vittorio. 'But I don't want them talking about me.'

He was hearing tiny alarm bells go off in his head. If he got involved in the publicity, it was doubtless that the headlines from a few years ago would feature again. Years ago, if the press ran a story that was untrue, they could be taken to court and sued. But the whole ethos of reporting had changed with the invention of social media. People saw and heard things and repeated them, with no thought to truth. Tracking people on the internet was an intense and relentless task—even if they were selling lies. Accounts were there one day and gone the next.

His mind drifted back to his ex. Alona was the star of new designer brand. She would hate their past relationship to be brought up now. He had no idea if she'd dealt with her addiction or not, he was just conscious that without meaning to, he could cause her further pain.

'I'd prefer not to be in any of the publicity,' he repeated.

'It might be a bit late for that,' sighed Jen, turning her tablet around again.

And there it was. A whole new hastily-thrown-together clip. Someone had identified him from the initial publicity, and someone else had captured a few clips of him and Sydney at the waterfalls. They were swimming, laughing, and sunbathing. There was nothing immediately concerning about the pictures. At first glance, they looked like friends. But anyone with half a brain could see the simmering attraction below the surface. There was one distinct shot where

Sydney was looking at him out of the side of her eyes, and that picture said a thousand words.

He could feel the heat rise at the back of his neck. He'd been there. They'd had fun. But he hadn't realised things had looked so obvious between them. Yes, there had been gentle flirting, but this?

'You've seen the graph,' said Jen quietly. 'This could make things really explode.'

He knew she was right. And he hated it. But the press hadn't really churned up the old stories; right now they just seemed interested in the new.

'She seems nice—Sydney, right?'

'Yes,' he replied, feeling strangely awkward.

'And you've had a chat?' enquired Jen.

'What do you mean?'

'Well, it's kind of obvious you're both not really looking for love.'

He breathed in slowly, wondering if he should actually admit to their agreement. 'We've reached an arrangement,' he said slowly. 'But I'm not sure she'd want that arrangement under the microscope.'

Jen walked across the office and nodded. 'It's a shame you didn't pick one of the social media types. They would have loved this.'

'Well, I didn't,' he said decidedly. 'Probably because they're not my type.'

He looked at the frozen frame from the last

video. The look on Sydney's face. It was like something fizzled down inside him. They might not be his type, but Sydney certainly was.

'She might not agree to be filmed,' he said quickly, not entirely sure how he would explain this to her.

Jen gave a casual smile that he realised was a lot more calculated than he would have liked. 'She answered a few questions earlier when a crew member asked how she was finding the cruise. She did it when she was shopping.'

'She was shopping,' he repeated blankly, trying to take all this in.

'Well,' said Jen, pulling a face, 'she didn't exactly shop, she just browsed. But Tara, our sales assistant, said she looked *magnificent* in a designer gown. I'm sure we could throw that in to persuade her to allow some casual photography this evening.'

'You think Sydney Scott can be bought with a gown?' He was disgusted at even the thought of that.

Jen moved near to him and bent down. 'Why don't you let me do the talking? I'll tell her it's all very casual. It won't impose at all on your normal dinner. And I'll let her know if she feels she doesn't have something appropriate for our exclusive restaurant, that we're happy to provide anything she needs with our compliments.' Jen gave a wave of her hand, 'We could do her hair and make-up, offer her some complimentary sessions at the spa at her leisure.'

Vittorio knew in a heartbeat he'd been played. Jen had already planned all this. After all, the whole love boat experience had been her brainchild. She had skin in this game. She wanted everything to work perfectly, and for the publicity to work in their favour.

'What restaurant are we going to?' The cruise ship had seven exclusive restaurants, all led by accomplished chefs.

'Whichever one she wants to go to,' said Jen promptly, leaving him with no doubt that she had all of this planned to perfection.

He gave a sigh. 'Okay, if Sydney agrees, then I'll go. Just let me know the time and the place.'

Jen beamed, turned, and set off. He only prayed that Sydney would actually agree to this without being offended.

Sydney walked across the restaurant in her glittering dress, her up-do from the cruise ship salon leaving a few tendrils of hair around her face and shoulders.

She'd even treated herself to a dark red lipstick from another cruise ship shop and was feeling like a million dollars.

Vittorio's eyes were wide as she sat down. 'Thanks for the dress,' she said, beaming.

He blinked, his eyes apparently overwhelmed by the glitter. 'Well, that certainly makes a statement.'

She nodded as the waiter poured some wine. 'You do know I initially said no to all this.'

He gave a half smile. 'I heard. I think the rest of the executive suite might have heard.'

Sydney tapped her fingers on the table. 'If you'd been a terrible date the other day, it would definitely have been a no.'

'Does that mean I was a good date?' She could see the spark in his eyes.

'I didn't say that.' She held up her hand. 'But just know I've had worse.' She lifted her glass to him. 'And you do know I have some conditions, don't you?'

'Apart from the glamourous wardrobe?'

She leaned forward and whispered conspiratorially, 'Actually, your chief arranger lady, she suggested the wardrobe and any hair and make-up I wanted to keep up the illusion.'

'She did?' He didn't let on that he knew Jen had masterminded the whole thing.

'She did. Now.' Sydney took a glance around her. 'Where's the camera?'

'It's to the side of us,' he said, without looking in that direction. 'Apparently if it doesn't have a complete view of our faces, it's more difficult for anyone on the internet to lip-read and say they know exactly what we're talking about.'

'I thought we were just being photographed.'

'It's what I initially agreed to. But then I realised that some of the social media gurus were livestreaming a few things, so I threw in some extra precautions.'

'Wow.' Sydney sat back for a moment, feeling sideswiped.

'What?'

She shook her head. 'I was almost treating this as some kind of joke. I didn't even consider things like that.'

The waiter appeared next to them and took their order quickly.

Vittorio looked at her steadily. 'We agreed for them to photograph us from afar. We didn't agree for them to know what we're saying.'

'Thank goodness,' she sighed. She glanced downwards and fingered the shimmering material of her dress. 'I guess everything comes with a cost.'

He looked serious. 'You do know that there will be a good chance you'll be identified through the media.'

She blinked. 'I'm not that interesting, Vittorio. I have no skeletons in my closet.'

He tilted his head to one side. 'None?'

She shrugged. 'Well, my first boyfriend replaced me with my roommate when I went on my first dig, and the second guy went to find himself, though I have no idea if he ever did. And my last disaster was a fiancé who is now married to his secretary and awaiting the birth of their first baby.' She held up both hands. 'So, no skeletons. No scandals. And this—' she smiled '—is why I'm only interested in men who have been dead for years, had the title of pharaoh, and are currently buried beneath the sands of Egypt. It makes life simpler.'

Now he pulled a face.

'What?' she asked.

'I'm almost afraid to go next,' he said.

She stopped and stared for a moment. 'Does that mean you have skeletons in your closet? Darn it, I knew I should have googled you.'

He looked a bit uncomfortable, and she stopped joking. All of a sudden, she realised he might have a dead wife or girlfriend in his past, something truly horrible, and she was joking about things.

'I've made headlines before,' he admitted.

'What did you do?'

He gave her an interesting look and shook his head. 'Why's your assumption that I did something?'

'Because if you make headlines, it's usually for a reason.'

He held up one hand. 'I dated someone famous. Things didn't go well, and when we parted, she gave a few interviews that didn't make me sound like boyfriend of the year.'

'Isn't that normal when people break up?'

'Probably. All I'm saying is, if you do go looking on the internet, don't believe everything you read.'

'Why would I read it when you can tell me?'

He gave a sad kind of smile. 'I don't want to betray a confidential aspect about someone else. But she implied things about me that just weren't true. She said I was controlling and—' he took a big breath '—she kind of hinted that I might have been abusive.' He held up one hand straight away. 'And that's absolutely not true.'

'Then why would she say it?' Sydney's stomach instantly clenched. Abusive? A sick feeling of dread flooded through her. It put her on edge straight away.

Vittorio shook his head and ran his fingers through his hair. 'She didn't actually say it. She just hinted. It's the press and the internet that did the rest.'

Sydney's heart rate started to calm down. She knew what the press could do. She wrinkled her nose. 'Who was she again?'

He met her gaze. 'Her name is Alona. She's a supermodel.'

It took Sydney a few moments to compute. She didn't really follow headlines about models, rock stars, or any of those kinds of people, but even she had heard of Alona.

'Isn't she a real party girl?'

He let out a sigh. 'Yes and no.'

Sydney frowned. 'You don't strike me as the party girl type.'

He leaned his head on his hand. 'I'm not, I guess I just thought I was—for about five minutes.'

Sydney leaned back in her chair and contemplated him. This was eye-opening, and a lot more than she'd bargained for. But…really? Did she believe the stories—that she hadn't even read yet? No, she didn't think so. Vittorio had never said or done anything that had given her cause for concern. But it all still put her guard up a little. She'd been burned before—she didn't need that again.

'You didn't say anything?'

'She had a number of other issues going on, and I think she probably wasn't in the best place.'

'You're being very diplomatic.'

'Am I? I didn't feel that way when I saw the headlines,' he admitted.

'But you didn't sue?'

He sighed. 'Reputation is everything, and it did feel damaging at the time. But—' he took a breath '—she didn't say specific things, she just implied them. Like I said—the internet just ran with them and people put their own spin on things.'

Her skin prickled. If he had a bad reputation, what would that mean for her and her position if she was associated with him?

This had all seemed like a joke when it had been put to her earlier—agreeing to continue to be in his company and to let the photographers snap them from afar. It had seemed harmless. But maybe it wasn't.

She worked in a country where women's rights weren't always respected. Although she'd been fortunate not to directly experience anything untoward, she generally always had people she worked with around about her as a layer of protection.

The waiter came and placed their food before them. It gave Sydney a moment to gather her thoughts. He'd just been honest with her. She looked at the man sitting across from her. Maybe he wasn't over his ex. Maybe he still loved her. But did Sydney have any concerns about being around him?

No. He'd been warm and friendly in her company, though the sizzle she felt when she looked at him? Maybe she should ignore that. Maybe she should just keep him in the category of personal tour guide.

She took a breath and lifted her glass as the waiter finished pouring their wine. 'So, we've been honest with each other. But I have one question.'

'What?'

'Were you a cheater?'

He blinked, clearly confused by the question. 'No, of course not. Why would you ask that?'

'Because we're being honest with each other and that's important to me. I don't like cheaters. I've experienced it before, and it doesn't sit well with me. And if you were a cheater, I'd likely reconsider our deal.'

The expression on Vittorio's face told her everything she needed to know. 'I'm not a cheater, never have been,' he said clearly. 'I'm also not the other things that were implied about me.'

She gestured for him to lift his glass. 'Then let's toast to this arrangement. It suits us both.' She looked down at the dress. 'I seem to have gained a beautiful dress out of this, and—' her blue gaze fixed on his '—if we continue to be honest with each other for the rest of the cruise, I don't think we will have any issues.'

The feeling of dread started to dissipate. She

wasn't judging him on past rumours. She was happy to continue the illusion.

He lifted his glass. 'So, my only competition is pharaohs who've been dead for thousands of years?'

She raised her eyebrows, 'But they are *tough* competition. You have a lot to live up to.'

'Got it,' he said, and clinked his glass against hers.

CHAPTER FIVE

THE CRUISE SHIP couldn't actually get any closer to the island of Santorini, so Sydney and Vittorio had to wait alongside the other guests for a tender to come and collect them.

'You do know that people think Atlantis is around here somewhere, don't you?' he said.

Sydney was leaning on the railing, admiring the tiny white houses with their blue roofs and the blue, lagoon-style water between the cruise ship and the island.

'You mean it isn't?' she asked breezily. 'Because this place looks exactly like where Atlantis should be.'

'Do you like the myths and legends?' asked Vittorio, intrigued to know a bit more about her. He loved that she'd pursued her dream with passion. And although her brother had been on the receiving end of some stinging comments, it was clear that they had a good relationship. He noticed she hadn't mentioned parents, which made him suspect that, like his, they were no longer around.

She tipped her head back, letting the sea breeze catch her hair. 'I love myths and legends. All of them. From the Minotaur to the Loch Ness Monster, the Trojan horse, and, of course, the finest of them all, Atlantis.'

'Do you think there's any truth in any of them?'

She laughed and put her hand on her heart. 'Oh, in here, they're all true. Though I'm a historian, a scientist, and I generally believe what science and the artefacts tell us, I like to be flexible enough to allow for some leeway in what people believe, and then there's the age-old fact that a lot of our own beliefs have changed due to modern discoveries.'

She leaned closer and whispered in his ear.

'And yes, I've watched every documentary, read every theory, and collected all the *National Geographic*s. It's nice to explore a legend and look for some truth in it.'

'So, you suspect there's another island around here, or that Santorini was the true capital of Atlantis and there's a whole lot buried under the sea.'

She smiled as one the crew gestured to them to move to the tender. 'It depends what day of the week it is.' She smiled. 'And how I'm feeling that day.'

* * *

By the time they crossed the water and landed onshore on the old port of Fira, the heat was starting to build. As a number of tenders had been used, the passengers all landed at different times.

Vittorio looked up towards the long queue which had already formed for the cable car, and the donkey trail which zig-zagged up the side of the hill. The steps were steep and several children were climbing onto the donkeys.

'How about a walk?' He smiled at her, glancing down at her shoes.

She looked up at the town at the top of the hill, the rest of the area scattered with the white houses with blue roofs that were famous on Santorini.

'As long as you promise there'll be something to drink up there.'

They started walking up the trail, dodging some donkeys that were coming down, and moving out the way of those who were climbing up. It only took a few minutes for Vittorio to reach out and offer his hand, which Sydney gladly accepted.

He tried not to smile. It had been a natural response, and she hadn't hesitated to take it. But was she feeling the same strange sensations that he was as their skin made contact? He couldn't actually remember the last time he had held hands with a woman. Not like this. Not when there was no relationship to speak of. But that didn't stop his heart from beating a little faster and a little pulse from shooting up his arm.

He'd noticed other men, and women, glancing at Sydney while they were together. She had a real natural beauty about her. Even in her casual clothes, with her natural curls falling around her face, the smattering of freckles across her nose, and her light tan, there was something about her that invited a second glance. Maybe it was those blue eyes that almost matched the colour of the lagoon that drew people in? He blinked and glanced away, not wanting to be caught staring.

After their conversation last night, Alona had drifted through his thoughts. Not in any romantic way. He hoped she was doing well and had things under control. For him, it had brought home the differences between Sydney and his past romantic partner. There were some similarities, of course—both were career driven, and both were intelligent. But Sydney's drive was different. Her passion was intriguing. The sparkle in her eyes when she spoke about what she loved touched him in a way he hadn't expected. But they'd barely scratched the surface with each other.

He wanted to know more. He wanted to find

out everything about her, and share the same with her. This fake dating had seemed like a convenient joke to begin with, but he was realising how much he valued the time they spent together. It was fun—something he hadn't had in a long time.

The climb was steeper than it looked, but there were lots of opportunities to stop and admire the view on the way. At one point, there was a shout above them, and they looked up to see a whole host of donkeys careening down towards them.

No, it was a stampede. And they were directly in its path. It was clear the donkeys weren't paying attention to see if their path was clear, and Vittorio didn't hesitate; he grabbed Sydney around the waist and pulled her towards him.

The donkey's rough hair came into contact with their skin, leaving dirty trails on Sydney's pale shorts. Her breath caught short and his fingers came into contact with the bare skin at her waist.

She started laughing at the near miss, bending over the wall they were next to and clinging onto it. 'Now, that would be a message to send Pete!' she laughed. 'Killed by stampeding donkeys in Santorini.'

He was still holding her. 'You okay?'

She turned her face, just inches from his now, her eyelids almost touching his skin. 'Let's just say I'll need that drink.' She smiled, still not moving out of his hold.

He looked upwards and gave a little tug at her waist. 'Let's move.'

She glanced up and stayed pressed against him as they moved to the middle of the path. The next set of donkeys looked as if they were leaning on the wall as they sped down the path, almost using it to steer themselves.

'This is like the wacky races,' she said, now changing her position but grabbing his hand again.

'The what?' he asked.

'You've never seen the cartoon? My mum and dad introduced me to it. It's old. But used to run on one of the children's channels. This weird collection of cartoon characters in crazy cars that used to race across America. Someone always got in trouble. They had to dodge and dive everywhere. This—' she held out her hand to the path in front '—is like a real-life version of that.'

He shook his head. 'I have never heard of the wacky races. But I'll look it up later.'

They continued trudging up the path. At one point, Vittorio did wish they'd just stood in the queue for the cable car. But, as he tugged his T-shirt from his back, he admitted to himself that the cable car journey would likely have been less fun.

'Have you ever done this before?' she asked.

'Been to Santorini?'

She nodded.

'Yes and no.'

'What does that mean?'

'It was only ever flying visits. Once, when I was twelve with family for a wedding. We were only here a few days, and at twelve, I didn't really appreciate the place. And then for business while we decided what ports we wanted to stop at, and to scope out the possibilities for passengers.'

He was actually starting to feel a bit out of breath at the incline of this hill and made up his mind to spend more time in the gym. The sweat was running down his back.

It was almost like she'd read his mind. 'Take your top off, it's stifling here.'

He shot her a sideways glance and she laughed. 'What? I've seen it all before, when we went swimming. You don't need to be shy around me.'

He dropped her hand, pulled his shirt over his head, then grabbed her hand back. 'Do you want to relieve yourself of any clothes?' he teased.

'No options,' she sighed. 'Just these shorts and this top.' She tugged at the loose-fitting yellow top adorned with flowers.

They'd almost reached the top, and they saw the other people who'd also climbed head straight to a clifftop café/bar overlooking the bay. The tables were sheltered by large umbrellas, and Vittorio was only too glad to guide Sydney over to a table and sit down.

The waiter was prompt, bringing them both some water initially then taking their order. Because they were at the top of the town, there was a welcome breeze around them.

Sydney leaned back in her seat and looked at the water again. 'This is the perfect view. It's the kind of place where you could sit and write kids' fairy stories.'

'As long as they feature Atlantis?'

She lifted her water glass towards him. 'As long as they feature Atlantis,' she repeated, giving him a broad smile.

'Ever thought of doing that?'

'Writing kids stories?' She shook her head. 'My imagination is just for myself. I'm more a factual person. I've been asked to contribute to factual children's books about Egypt, and I've been happy to do that.'

'So, you're an author as well as an Egyptologist?'

She gave him a soft smile. 'Egypt opens a world of doors. I'm an Egyptologist, a researcher, a tour guide, a supervisor of master of science dissertations, in charge of digs, an assistant museum curator, and whatever else I get asked to do. It's never just one thing.'

He nodded, then bent forward a little. He was still curious about her. 'Your name, it's unusual. You're from England, right?'

The expression she gave him made him realise this had been brought up a number of times before. She sighed, but that changed to a look of relief as the waiter set down two cold beers in front of them.

'I'd love to tell you I had an ancient grandparent called Sidney and they named me after the female version.'

He took the hint. 'But?'

'But—' she gave her hair a shake '—but I had *that* set of parents, that decided to name their children after where they were conceived.'

He started laughing. 'No.'

'Oh yes,' she replied, shaking her head. 'So, they were in Australia, and I guess I could have been named after places a whole lot worse than Sydney.'

Now he was intrigued. 'Like what?'

She took a sip of her beer. 'Oh, I researched. Australia has places called Foul Bay, Useless Loop, Mount Monster, and Disaster Bay.' She lifted her beer to him. 'So, I guess I got lucky.'

'I guess you did.' Then he frowned. 'Wait, what about Pete, then?'

She grinned. 'This is the part of the story I do like. Pete was conceived in Peterhead, a town in Scotland. And it could have been worse. He could have got Auchtermuchty.' She emphasized the syllables, *Och-ter-much-ty.* 'Or Ballachulish—*Baall-a-hoolish.*' She was watching his expression while she did her best Scottish accent. 'There's more,' she said, still smiling.

He raised one hand. 'I bet there is, but that's enough.' He leaned back, sipping his own beer. 'And it makes me immensely grateful to be named after my great-grandfather.'

'What did he do?' she asked quickly.

'Clothes. He was a mastrosarto, a master tailor. He was critical of every suit he ever saw, unless it had been cut by his own team of tailors. He could glance at someone thirty feet away and tell you who made their suit.'

'Wow,' she said, obviously impressed.

'I'm just sorry he's not around now to tell me where he wants me to buy my suits. I'm not sure they would all be up to his standards.'

'That's a nice history.'

'It is. He died when I was around seven, so I never really got to appreciate him as much as I would have liked.'

He watched her draw in a deep breath and look out across the lagoon again. 'That's just it,' she said. 'We don't write things down. We don't always capture the moments because we don't realise things might be happening for the last time.' It was as if a cold breeze just captured her, because he could see the prickles rise on her skin, and she wrapped her arms around herself. 'We think we'll always have them and then, one minute, we don't.'

He heard it. That little break in her voice. He couldn't help himself—he stood up and walked around the table, sitting down in the chair next to her and wrapping an arm around her shoulders.

She didn't speak. She didn't have to. He could sense the small shake in her arms and shoulders. So, he spoke for her. 'Losing people we love is always hard. Sometimes it's sudden and you don't get a chance to say goodbye. Sometimes we do know it's imminent, but then we might have to watch them suffer, which is a whole other sort of grief.'

She looked up at him in surprise, and he could see unshed tears in her eyes.

'Both have the same outcome, and neither way seems fair,' he said simply, and she nodded.

She turned her head and fixed her eyes on the ocean. 'This is why I prefer the myths and legends sometimes,' she said. 'It takes away from the reality check of life.'

'We can't get away from real life. If we could, I'd get away from taxes, business dealings, complaints, staffing issues, and people who want an instant return on their investments. Though I think I would like to imagine living in Atlantis instead.'

She gave a sigh and put her head on his shoulder. If she didn't want to talk about things, he wouldn't push her. It was none of his business, and this was obviously something that was quite raw.

The waiter came back over and Vittorio ordered them coffees this time around, and they stayed in the same position for a while.

He noticed the photography crew in the distance at one point, but because they didn't approach them, he saw no reason for concern. He was quite happy just to stay here, with this idyllic view and his arm around a beautiful woman.

He actually couldn't even remember the last time he'd spent a few hours relaxing. If he wasn't working, he was at the gym, dealing with family issues, or sometimes even sleeping.

Even sitting here, his brain was going into overdrive about his latest to-do list, and he consciously pushed the thought away. Nothing was urgent. Everything could wait. And his brain was starting to acknowledge what other people had been telling him for a while. He needed to delegate more tasks.

He already had a fabulous personal assistant, and good staff who worked in other specific areas for him. But he also had staff who could probably be promoted beyond their current positions.

Jen was a good example. The whole love boat launch had been her idea, and while she had a general role as cruise director for their newest ship, her background degree was in business management and marketing. She was capable of a whole lot more. Maybe, if this whole thing was a success, he could look at creating a new role for her that might mean he could delegate some of his workload.

The coffees arrived and he could feel Sydney start to settle. She was breathing easier, and the tiny trembles had stopped. He was glad now they'd chosen to walk up the donkey trail. Santorini had an abundance of history involving the Minoan, Roman and Greek civilisations. He imagined that Sydney might have wanted to visit some of the ruins at Akrotiri or the museum at Thera, but due to the popularity of Santorini, and the fact that the cruise ship's allotted time period was only a few hours, further exploration was probably impossible.

She gave him a nudge. 'Are we walking back down, or taking the cable car?'

The queue for the cable car to get back down was just as big as it had been at the foot of the hill. 'Are you brave enough?' he teased.

'Absolutely,' she said. 'I'll take some more pictures on the way down. Prove to Pete that I've at least left my cabin on one occasion.'

'You didn't send him pictures of the falls?'

'No.' She smiled. 'I was still mad at him for sending me on the love cruise. I let him think I was hiding out in my cabin.'

Vittorio smiled. 'There's a little bit of wickedness inside you, isn't there?'

'When it comes to my brother, absolutely.'

'Did you bully him when you were kids?'

She didn't look offended and took a few moments to answer. 'We bullied each other. He broke my arm at one point, and I pushed him out of a tree and broke his shoulder. We were pretty even.'

'What did your mum say?'

Something flashed across her eyes. 'She said we had a season ticket for A&E. She kept wondering if someone from social services would visit because we were there that often. But our local doctor knew us and knew exactly what we were like. He even sent us home one day when he caught us trying to build a rope swing across our nearby river.'

'Trouble?' asked Vittorio with a smile.

'With a capital *T*,' she agreed. Then she tilted her head to one side. 'I can't imagine that you were the model child either.'

He gave a little shrug. ‘I didn’t have siblings, but I had plenty of cousins, so my mother liked to think that they led me astray. The police found me under a car with a kitchen knife one night when I’d arranged to meet my cousins and play—’ he tried to think of a word that would be equivalent to the Italian one ‘—commandos?’

‘And where were they?’

He laughed. ‘Oh, tucked up in bed. I was the only one foolish enough to go out at midnight.’

‘I can imagine your mother’s face.’

He nodded. ‘Oh, she was mortified—but clearly it was all my older cousins’ idea. I was just the innocent bystander.’

‘Did you get away with things like that?’

He smiled. ‘Every time. The joy of being an only child.’

She straightened a little and gave him a serious look. ‘But did you grow up not taking responsibility for any of your actions?’

‘Oh, don’t worry. I got into trouble on plenty of occasions when things couldn’t be blamed on anyone else. I was just a normal kid.’

‘So, how did you get into boats?’

He smiled. ‘I told you earlier about my degree, and the work placement I did. I was lucky. It was a new, developing cruise company. I was able to see from start to finish the whole commissioning, designing, and building of a cruise ship. I’m not sure where else I could have got that experience, and it just started a love for the industry for me. As soon as I was able, I bought into the company, and the rest, as they say, is history.'

'So, you didn't want to be a master tailor?'

He sighed. 'I think that profession had more or less finished by the time I was a boy. I had to look at something new, something for myself.'

He settled the bill, and they stood to walk back to the donkey trail. 'What do you say to people who hate cruises?' she teased.

He lifted his finger and pointed at her. 'I say that there is a cruise for everyone. You just need to find *your* cruise.'

As they started down the trail, he turned to take her hand again. The trail was just as hazardous going down as it had been going up. 'You must have cruises on the Nile.'

'We do,' she agreed, 'but they are much smaller boats.'

'The Nile isn't deep enough for the cruise ships that are used in the Med. It's a totally different style of ship. It all depends on where a cruise might be sailing. It could be around Iceland, the Nordic countries, the Bahamas, or across the Atlantic. Each cruise ship will be designed to withstand those conditions and be best suited to those areas.'

There was a familiar noise behind them, and

they both automatically moved sideways, avoiding another rush of donkeys.

There were more ship passengers walking near them, the downwards descent clearly having more appeal than the uphill ascent had. But several had underestimated the trip, and Sydney and Vittorio quickly separated to take the arms of an elderly couple.

He watched her slip one arm around the older woman and help steer her down the path, saving her from several missteps while he did the same with her husband. The older man was puffing and panting by the time they reached the bottom, and Vittorio gave instructions to his crew to supervise the couple on the way back to the ship, and to ask the medical staff to check in on them later.

'You're really just a soft touch, aren't you?' Sydney smiled up at them as they crossed on their own tender.

He pulled a face. 'Depends entirely on the time and place.' He looked back at the island they'd just left. 'For that couple, yes. But—' he gave her a cheeky look '—if I find out you discover Atlantis and don't let me in on the discovery, then you'll find out I'm not always a soft touch. I'll play hardball for equal rights there.'

She leaned on the railing of the tender. 'Oh, I think the Atlantis I'll find will have women in charge.' She gave him a sideways grin. 'I might not even let you on the island.'

'That seems cruel. Okay then, what if I start my own dig in Egypt and find a pharaoh's tomb and don't let you see it?'

Her gaze narrowed. 'I can be very unreasonable,' she said in a calm voice.

He leaned back against the railing, watching her with mischief in his gaze. 'Oh, I bet you can be.'

She flicked her curls back from her face and counted off on her fingers. 'Well, let's just say you got the funding, and the permissions, and the dig team, and the agreement with the university.'

'You're making it sound like so much fun,' he quipped.

She held up a finger. 'And you forget—I have previous experience with pharaohs. They don't like intruders. I might just arrange to curse you.'

She said it in such a flyaway manner that he actually believed her.

'You can communicate with the dead?' he joked.

And that was it. The moment she froze and the fun left her face. He knew instantly he'd said something wrong.

He waited a few seconds, slipping his arm around her waist. Her head went to his shoulder, just as it had before. If they hadn't been that close, he would have missed the whispered words. 'I wish I could.'

CHAPTER SIX

THE CRUISE SHIP docked early at Sorrento and the whole ship was abuzz with activity. There was a world of possibilities for the passengers at this port, the chance to visit the actual city of Sorrento, the beautiful island of Capri, or to take the journey to the world-famous ruins of Pompeii.

Like at the previous port, the ship ran a number of tenders to take the passengers to land and co-ordinate everything from there.

Vittorio was nervous. After they'd reached the ship last night, Sydney had made her excuses to get away. He'd known not to chase after her but had taken a casual stroll around the many restaurants last night and hadn't seen her in any. She hadn't been visible in any of the bars either. He could always have knocked on the door of her cabin, but that felt intrusive. He'd only go to her cabin if she asked him to.

Finally he'd spotted her and felt an immense wave of relief. But he hadn't approached. She'd been wearing a loose, animal print dress and talking to an elderly couple, whom he'd recognised as the two they'd helped on the donkey trail.

She'd been laughing with them, and that was enough for him. He'd had no reason to go over and try to join in, so he'd left to go and do some work.

He'd taken a guess at what she'd want to do today, but still hadn't had the chance to check.

As he walked down the stairs to the place passengers were directed to meet the tenders, he could see her already waiting. She wore a wide-brimmed hat, a bright green dress, and thick-soled sandals. He moved beside her and put his arm around her waist. 'Okay?'

She met his gaze with a slightly tempered smile. 'Okay,' she repeated, then looked down at her dress. 'I wore this so you won't lose me in the crowds at Pompeii.'

'You think it will be that busy?'

'I think it's always that busy. I think it should have made it on to the New Seven Wonders of the World list.'

He frowned. 'What? And bump the Colosseum off?'

'No,' she said reasonably. 'We're keeping that, and Petra. We can debate the others at a later date. They all have merit. Maybe we should just expand the list to eight.'

They moved to a tender and Vittorio was glad he'd ordered a separate car for them. There were ten buses for the passengers going to Pompeii alone, and there were other cruise ships in the vicinity. It would be a busy day.

This time he'd prepared and asked the driver to get them some iced coffees for the journey, and the limo had a fridge that was filled with water and sodas.

'Is this somewhere you can actually show me around? How many times have you been here?'

'Four,' he said easily. 'What about you?'

'Three,' she said, pulling a face, clearly annoyed he'd beaten her.

'At least Mount Vesuvius has more or less stopped smoking. I heard they stopped the visits for a few days.'

'They did,' he confirmed. 'Imagine if you'd come on holiday and this was your dream destination and you had to miss it because of the ash.'

She gave a shudder as she sipped her coffee. 'Imagine if it actually ever fully erupts again. All that they've found will likely be lost and completely destroyed.'

'They say the phase of heightened activity since the eruption in 1944 was unusually long. They think it might have concluded.'

'But what about the ash the other day?'

'Apparently they are saying the area is safe, and they're not worried.'

She put a hand to her chest. 'I would have been devastated if we couldn't come here today. I actually couldn't sleep last night thinking about it.'

It was the first genuine smile he'd seen from her today and it warmed his heart. It was nice to see her passion for her work in action.

'It's a big site, and I've arranged a private tour guide, but is there anything in particular you want to spend time on?'

'Everything,' she admitted. 'The villas, the Roman baths, the forum, the amphitheatre.'

'Just as well I brought my walking shoes then,' he joked.

The drive along the coast was pleasant, and as soon they stepped from the limo, they could feel the heat of the day already building.

He looked at her lightly tanned skin. 'You got sunscreen?'

'Already on.' She swished her dress. 'And part of the reason I wore this dress. It covers most areas.'

And it did. He knew that was a good thing as she put her large hat on her head.

They stood in the queue with the rest of the crowds. Vittorio could have asked for special treatment, but Pompeii wasn't a private site. It was a public place for people across the world to see the devastation caused by the eruption. While he was happy to buy tickets online to save some time queueing, he had a belief that everyone should be equal at a place like this.

As they entered the site, he heard Sydney take in a deep breath. There was something about a place like this. The history, the loss of life, the memories left behind.

They started through the Stabian Gate, which gave them a good view of the city walls. Sydney couldn't resist touching it. 'Isn't it amazing,' she said, with wonder in her eyes, 'that even today we still don't really understand how people did some of these things, thousands of years ago. We still debate how the pyramids were built, how they managed to erect the Great Wall of China, and then we look at how straight and well-constructed city walls like these are, and wonder how, in our day and age, we haven't really managed to better their workmanship and techniques.'

Vittorio couldn't help but smile. This was her in her element, and he felt honoured to see it.

The guide led them into the city. The streets, while mainly straight, were often uneven and difficult to traverse. In their own day, they would have been the height of modern technology. The pavements were high, with large volcanic stones for crossing at spots—to save the shoes and clothes of foot travellers, mainly because mud, waste, and floods frequently flowed down the streets. What was most obvious were the deeply grooved wheel tracks from the constant flow of traffic along those streets. 'Can you imagine the smell?' He wrinkled his nose as Sydney and he made their way along, trying the stepping stones.

They made their way to the gladiator training arena and barracks, listening while the guide told them the gladiators were slaves, and slept in tiny rooms on the ground floor of buildings. The stone walls were still there, with the notches in the walls where the wooden beams would have been to create the second floor.

When they reached the large amphitheatre, built into the hill, Sydney stood in the middle and spun around with her arms wide open. 'Just think,' she exclaimed with a wide smile on her face, 'people actually performed where we're standing.'

She took a few steps towards the seats. 'Just imagine five thousand people watching a tragedy or comedy here. The atmosphere. The noise.'

'The smell,' he added with a laugh, then drew his fingers across some of the seats, which still had numbers carved into them. 'It's amazing to think that class is still as big an issue today as it was then.' The guide had told them that the more important a citizen was, the closer they got to sit to the stage.

As the exited the amphitheatre, they wondered at the ancient fast-food outlets nearby. Stones built areas, with a space for round pots in the countertops. 'We haven't changed that much really, have we?' Sydney asked as she ran her fingers around the space for the pots.

Some of the rest of the site passed in a whirl. The temples of Pompeii, the drainage system again, the ancient loaf of bread that could still be found in the bakery. The holes in the kerb stones where traders could tie up their donkeys and carts.

The heat was rising again, and they stopped in a shaded part so Sydney could fan herself with her hat and they could take a few minutes to drink some water.

'Wouldn't you like to go back?' he asked. 'Even if just for five minutes, to glimpse the people, see the crowded streets, see it all in actual life?'

'You mean like a time machine moment?'

'Exactly,' he said. 'Wouldn't it be spectacular?'

She let out a long, slow breath as she contemplated the question. 'I read a whole fiction series where a bunch of historians could go back in time and watch real-life events but not interfere.' She shook her head. 'There have been TV shows like that too, and it never works out well, does it?'

'Because we always want to interfere?' he asked.

She nodded. 'It's the sadness. The inevitability. And while I would love to watch five minutes, it would damage me.' She ran her fingers through her curls. 'I would see those people, those children, those faces, and know what would happen to them. I think it would actually kill me.'

He reached over and took her hand. 'Your heart is too big. I'm offering you a chance to time travel and you can't get over the ethics.'

She smiled as she laid her other hand over his. 'It's the same when I think about Egypt. Whether or not I'd like to go back and see it too.' She blew some curls out of her face. 'And while I'd love it from a historical point of view, I know I would see the slaves being treated so badly. Being whipped, being starved, being killed. My head couldn't cope with that.'

Their guide gave them a nod, and they carried on to other parts of the city, looking at mosaics depicting war, religion or sometimes just daily life.

He took them into one of the Pompeii brothel's small, cramped rooms, where the mosaics on the walls depicted almost a menu of carnal activity. Sydney gave a sigh. 'Another aspect of life that hasn't changed in thousands of years. People are still used in the sex trade.'

She turned to him as they walked out of the brothel.

'Imagine if aliens landed and looked at all our history, and our present day. We still have wars, famine, drought, and sex work.'

Vittorio nodded. 'If the aliens had any sense, they would probably turn and just fly away again.' He arched his eyebrows. 'Maybe they already have?'

She laughed and slid her arm into his as they carried along the streets. Vittorio could sense how easy they were around each other now. He still found her attractive in every way possible, and it was hard not to act on it.

Even now, the feel of her skin against his just seemed as if it were meant to be. It had been a long time since he'd felt a connection like this, and it was all just so random.

What if he hadn't stayed on the boat? What if her brother hadn't booked her on this cruise? What if she'd refused to have a holiday and decided to stay in Egypt? There were so many scenarios where they would just never have met. And that made him distinctly uncomfortable. Because he was glad to have met Sydney Scott. He was glad to have this chance to get to know her.

They continued to tour the city, and their guide filled them with a host of facts that he'd never known, or might have forgotten from previous trips. Sydney asked an array of interesting questions, but her biggest point of interest was around the third of the site that had yet to be excavated. Pompeii was still partially buried and a world of possibilities.

'You're almost itching to get in there,' he said in her ear as they looked at where work was still being carried out.

'I absolutely am,' she agreed, looking up at him with those intelligent blue eyes. 'Aren't you?'

He smiled and laughed. 'I'm not in a hurry to spend my time with tiny brushes and tools, inching away at the soil,' he said. 'But I wouldn't mind looking at the final results.'

'But it's a big debate,' she sighed, 'on whether to continue, or use concerted efforts to preserve and maintain what's already been discovered.' She swept out her arms. 'And look at it, it's marvellous already.'

'It is,' he agreed, and they made their way along to the area that revealed the most prestigious private homes. Most contained further frescos and mosaics; others featured beautiful gardens with private baths and running water.

'The technology they had all those thousands of years ago is remarkable,' said Vittorio, trying to keep everything straight in his head.

As their guide left them, Sydney turned towards him. 'The best is yet to come.' She slid her arm out and clasped his hand as she led him to what she called her favourite part.

'This is the Villa of Mysteries.' She smiled as they entered the building. The triclinium had three walls with a remarkably bright and vibrant painting covering its surface and a dark red background.

'Look at the colours,' said Vittorio. 'It's amazing that this has been preserved.'

They walked around, examining the level of detail. The walls were seventeen metres long and three metres high. It really was impressive. The paintings depicted a mystery ritual in ten sequences, showing Dionysus and his bride Ariadne in the central part.

'What's their story again?' he asked.

'Something around a cult, wine, dancing, claiming Ariadne as his bride, with possible use of psychoactive ingredients in the wine.'

He laughed. 'Has nothing changed in our cultures? We still have some of that too.'

The crowds around them had dissipated, and

there were only a few other people nearby. 'This is my favourite room in this place.' She smiled. 'A world of imagination and possibilities.'

She laid her head on his arm and they just stood for a few moments. Then she moved again, turning to face him and putting both hands at his waist. 'Thank you for bringing me here today. It's been a long time, and it's brought back lots of good memories and hope for the future.'

She was only inches from him, her nose just beneath his. And Vittorio moved, his lips brushing against hers. It was the lightest of touches but as he made it, Sydney moved her arms up around his neck.

They were in a public place, surrounded by history. But it seemed entirely natural to him. Their kiss deepened a little. Her scent filled his nostrils, light, with tones of amber, and every time he inhaled it was all her. Her lips were soft and willing against his, and when he pulled back, she was smiling at him.

He kept his voice low. 'I didn't overstep?' He had to ask.

They'd agreed to fake date. They'd agreed to get each other out of any of the dating rituals on the ship. But this was so much more. His feelings for her had deepened in a way he hadn't expected, but he had to be sure she was fine about this.

'No,' she said easily. 'We'll try that again someplace else.'

He could swear that his heart just soared in his chest, even though he knew that was physically impossible. But that small act centred him. The attraction between them had been slowly building, but this cemented things in his head—Sydney was as interested in him as he was in her. Maybe this fake dating thing was going to work out better than he'd ever thought?

He slung one arm around her shoulders, and they continued to stroll through the city, conscious that their day was soon coming to an end.

They continually caught sight of other familiar faces, and the extra photography crew who'd joined the ship. This was one of the most popular destinations for cruise ship passengers, so it was no wonder they had come along. They could see them chatting to several of the couples who'd they'd noticed in other settings, and several people who looked slightly awkward around each other and had obviously been paired up for the day.

Vittorio was relieved they weren't in that position.

As they passed a storage area with gates and a large number of shelves, he noticed a glass cabinet pushed back from immediate view.

He recognised it immediately and stopped

walking. It was the white plaster casts that had been made of people who'd been found in the aftermath.

Sydney stopped too and took a breath. They both knew that these tragic figures, intertwined together in their last moments, had been moved because of the recent unnecessary tradition of people taking a selfies with these poor people and posting them on social media.

It had turned into almost a spectator sport, instead of telling the solemn and tragic story it was supposed to tell the public, of the last moment of the citizens of Pompeii. 'I remember seeing this on one of my earlier trips,' he said softly.

'Me too,' she said, her fingers touching the thick metal of the gate.

'They did more work on the family of four that they found,' said Sydney. 'Do you remember them? Found beneath a staircase?'

He nodded.

'They found DNA and say that the remains presumed to be the mother was actually those of a man, and that he wasn't related to the two children found.'

'It's all so fascinating. Technology is changing so much of what we believe.'

Her eyes glittered as she looked at him. 'Yip, dinosaurs have feathers.'

Vittorio jolted and then almost doubled over

with laughter at the sudden subject change. He straightened up and put his arm around her. 'And you just keep surprising me,' he said.

It had been a wonderful day and Sydney was trying not to pinch herself in an effort to make sure it had actually happened.

Pompeii was wonderful, exactly as she'd remembered and still evoking all the magical memories and feelings. Then there had been the kiss.

The flirting had still been there, and the fact they'd been linking arms and holding hands had seemed entirely natural to her. When she'd turned to face him in her favourite place in Pompeii, it was like a message had been sent from somewhere.

As soon as his face had bent towards her, she'd responded. It had been so easy to snake her hands around his neck and pull him towards her, feeling those taut muscles against hers. The touch of his lips had been exactly what she'd wanted.

She knew neither of them had signed up for this. But she didn't care. At that second, she'd wanted it, and it had seemed so natural. Maybe it was time to change the rules of their fake dating?

Sydney could barely remember her last kiss. But this one she would never forget. Not just because of the place, but because of the person, and the sensations. It would have been perfect, except, nothing could progress further and that was probably for the best.

They'd drifted back through Pompeii and driven back to the ship, quenching their thirst with the waters and sodas they'd kept stored in the limo. It had been a long day, and when they'd reached the ship, Vittorio had invited her to dinner again.

'Not dinner,' she said, seeing the immediate disappointment on his face. She gave him a smile. 'Can we just do drinks and something light? Because of how hot it's been, I'm not too hungry.'

So, they agreed to meet in the executive lounge in an hour's time. There was no chance someone could do her hair and make-up, and she looked longingly at the silver dress before picking a different, shorter dress and a pair of heels.

Heels weren't somcthing she wore often, mainly just because of the nature of her job and how little time she had off. She smiled as she slid them on. Just because she didn't wear them often didn't mean that she couldn't.

She glanced in the mirror and did a quick double take. A quick wash and dry of her hair had her pulling out the straighteners. They were top of the range, and literally slid through her sectioned curls in seconds, leaving iron-straight hair. She looked quite different, and it made her laugh.

When she walked into the executive lounge, she saw Vittorio sitting at the bar, chatting to one of the barmen.

He didn't recognise her until she was right next to him, and she laughed as he did his own double take.

'What did you do?' he asked.

She slid her fingers through her hair. 'Decided to try something different.' She slid onto the bar stool next to him as a small plate of appetisers landed in front of her.

'What do you want to drink?' he asked.

Sydney smiled at the barman. 'I'll have a glass of rosé please.'

She waited until her glass was filled and then lifted it to Vittorio's bottle of beer. 'Are we toasting a successful day in Pompeii?'

His eyebrows gave the tiniest arch. 'In more ways than one,' he replied as they clinked their drinks together.

She smiled and took a sip of her wine, and then a nibble of the chicken in front of her. 'It was a great day. If you could just rearrange the whole schedule and let us book there tomorrow again, that would be great.'

'You think I can do that?'

She winked at him. 'There's got to be some benefit to hanging around with the chief executive.'

'Hanging around?' His eyebrows were lifted in amusement.

She just smiled.

'But that would mean you would miss out on Rome. Is that what you want?'

She groaned and put her head on the bar for a second. 'No, I want to do the gladiator tour and stand in the arena at the Colosseum. I want to see St Peter's again. I want to stand at the Roman Forum.'

'You don't want much, do you?' he teased.

She sighed. 'Take me to Rome.'

'Your wish is my command,' he joked.

She saw a hand waving and looked over, noticing the elderly couple she'd spoken to the other day, so she waved back, then asked the barman if she could buy them a few drinks.

'Who is that?'

'Oh, that's Jim and Mary. We met them in Santorini?'

He gave a nod of recognition.

'They asked me to have afternoon tea with them one day. I'm looking forward to it.'

'So, Jim is my competition?' he joked.

She looked over at them both and smiled. 'Oh, don't worry, I'm pretty sure Mary could take me, if she thought I was after Jim. They are hopelessly devoted to each other.'

He watched her watching them and could see something in her expression. A longing almost, and he wondered why.

Then something struck him. 'Hey. They're the oldest couple I've seen on this ship. Did they meet here?'

She shook her head, smiling widely. 'No, but theirs is the best story. They were booked on another cruise for the week before. But Jim had surgery and his travel agent rebooked their cruise without really checking the details.'

'They're here by mistake?' Vittorio's eyes were wide, and he felt a tiny wave of panic at the error. 'Are they unhappy about it?'

She laughed. 'No, they're having the time of their lives. Once they realised the mistake, they started making bets on certain couples. Mary has also picked out a few women who she thinks will never be happy with what they find. She heard them talking in one of the bars.'

Vittorio was shaking his head. 'Who needs social media when we have Mary.'

Sydney's phone pinged and she gave a start before glancing at the screen. It was Pete. Who is this? the text read, alongside an accompanying photo.

Sydney frowned and opened the message, giving a little gasp when she saw the photo. Someone had captured them in the Villa of Mysteries, and it was just that moment when they were looking at each other, before they kissed. It didn't actually matter that they weren't kissing in the photo as their intent was written all over their faces.

She gave a wry smile and turned the photo to Vittorio. 'My brother wants to know who you are.'

He took the phone and shook his head at the photo. 'Who on earth took that? I know there was a photography crew, but they weren't anywhere near us.'

She shrugged. 'Does it matter?'

His face was serious. 'Does it matter to you?' he asked.

'We agreed to fake date,' she said slowly, testing the water.

He looked at her carefully. 'Are you worried about it becoming more?'

She shook her head. 'Not at all. Unless you're secretly married with a family somewhere that are about to come out of the woodwork.'

His head shook too. 'No secret family.' Something came over his face. 'Ah, I think I might guess where this came from.'

She sipped her wine and leaned her head on one hand. 'Where?'

'Jen told me that some of the crew were "helping" the photographers and taking pictures of couples. Most of the world doesn't know who I am, but the ship's crew would. If they're off duty, some of the crew can go along to some of the day trips. I guess that's what happened.'

She wrinkled her nose and looked at him. 'They wouldn't be scared about upsetting the boss? What happens if you don't like having your picture taken?'

He gave a sigh. 'I don't really. But we live in a world of social media. I can't exactly complain, and I'm not going to get a crew member into trouble for a photo being taken in a public place.'

'Aren't you the good boss.' She smiled, one of her fingers tracing along his bare arm.

Their eyes connected. 'You're okay with this?' he reiterated.

'What is this?' she asked, holding his gaze.

'I don't know,' he admitted, then lowered his voice a little. 'But I'd like to find out.'

'Me too,' she said, then took a breath. 'But we've only known each other a short time.'

He nodded at her phone. 'And if your brother hadn't booked this cruise, we would never have met at all.'

She gave a soft smile. 'I'll need to thank him for that.'

He gave an equally soft smile, 'Yes, you will.'

Sydney gave a sigh. ‘There’s not much time on a cruise. It goes past so quickly.’

He nodded. ‘It does.’

She licked her lips. ‘So, it means we have a time limit.’

‘Do we?’

The way he asked the question made her stomach clench.

‘Maybe I want to visit Egypt sometime,’ he said casually.

Her skin prickled. She hadn’t been looking to meet anyone. She had sworn off men. This had been the last thing on her radar.

But somehow? She knew she wanted it. She knew she wanted to see what ‘this’ was. He was Italian; she was an English girl in Egypt. Their lifestyles and jobs were miles apart, but that didn’t mean things couldn’t work.

‘That might be nice,’ she said, almost embarrassed to meet his gaze again. Nerves washed over her. She’d been so adamant in the past that it was hard to admit that she was willing to take a chance again. A chance on someone that she barely even knew and had met on the ridiculous love boat.

If she’d been repeating this story to someone else, she would completely understand if they shook their head. But being in this moment was indescribable. Her body felt in tune with his.

Although she was capable of rational thought, she didn't want to be.

This was where she wanted to be. This was the moment she wanted to be in. This was the person she wanted to be with.

Right now, she might even send Pete and Jess to their dream destination next year, because there was no way she was getting off this boat in the near future. He could win the bet. And she would let him celebrate it.

'Will it be a problem that I'm actually alive and breathing?' he said in her ear, his breath tickling her skin.

'Oh, I think in these circumstances, I can forgive you for that.' Her face had turned to his and they were practically touching.

'I was kind of hoping that we could pick up where we left things earlier.'

'Where did we leave things?' She ran her finger down his arm again, knowing that she was likely driving him crazy.

'I think we left them about here.' His finger lifted her chin towards him and they kissed again. Last time had been a test. A way to make sure they were both on the same page. This time it had intent, a purpose.

She happily slid her arms around his neck again. He was subtle about kissing her. Keeping it light, and delicate, teasing almost. Her body shifted naturally towards his as she longed to feel him against her.

'It's those shoes,' he growled. 'Haven't seen you in high heels before.'

'Wait till you see me out of them.' She laughed in his ear.

His hands ran through her hair, and he stopped and gave it a little tug. 'I still like the curls. But this will do.'

'Will it?' Her teeth connected with his earlobe and he gave a low growl.

'It's time for us to be somewhere a little less public.'

She rested her forehead against his and grinned. 'Your place, or mine?'

'Whichever is closer.'

'I have no idea where your cabin is,' she admitted with a laugh, realising how ridiculous this all was.

Vittorio turned to the bar, spoke to the bartender, and signed something before clasping her hand firmly and leading her out of the bar.

The executive suite housed a number of cabins. Sydney's was only a few minutes away, but it seemed that Vittorio's was even closer.

He pushed the dark wood door open, led her inside, and closed the door firmly behind him.

Her arms were back around him straight away. She wasn't interested in how magnificent the cabin was. She didn't care about the view. She certainly didn't care about the thread count of the sheets. All that counted was the bed.

His fingers danced along the zipper of her dress. 'You sure about this?' he asked, his voice so low she could barely hear him.

'Absolutely,' she said, leaning up against the length of his body, and forgetting about everything else.

CHAPTER SEVEN

Rome rolled around with Sydney caught up in the tangle of Vittorio's sheets. His phone ringing sharply had awakened them both. She hated the way he peeled his body away from hers when he answered the phone.

'What?'

She sat up, hearing the concern in his voice.

'And what's the solution?'

She could hear murmuring at the end of the phone, followed by whole host of other questions from Vittorio. None of it sounded particularly good. 'Notify the passengers, let them know what's going on and what our plan will be.'

In the meantime, she was still trying to sort things out in her head. They'd stepped over the line with kissing—but last night? That had been a whole other ballgame.

How many fake dating relationships ended up like this?

Her head really didn't want to go there. Last night had been instinct, for both of them. They were consenting adults. They could do whatever they wanted to. But what was her hope for the end of this? Her brain just wouldn't let her go there right now, because she wasn't entirely sure.

'What is it?' she asked as soon as he ended the call.

He sat for a moment at the side of the bed, his fingers running through his hair, before standing up and giving her a weary smile. 'It's cruising,' he sighed.

She stood up, wrapping the sheet around her. 'What does that mean?'

He shook his head. 'Cruising is like the biggest jigsaw puzzle in the world. The ship that is currently in our berth at our next stop—Monte Carlo—has engine problems and won't be able to move today to free up the spot for us tomorrow. We're going to have to remain moored here at Rome overnight.'

'Doesn't that throw off your whole schedule?' She frowned. 'Isn't there somewhere else you can dock there?'

He shook his head. 'Not all ships are built the same. Where we dock all depends on the depth and size of the port, and the ships around us. There isn't another suitable berth for us to dock at.'

She sat down at a round table she hadn't even noticed before, next to the glass doors out to the balcony. 'This isn't good for your maiden voyage, is it?'

He shook his head. 'Nope. But I can count on one hand how often this happens. Cruise companies tend to keep their ships in good working order, because of precisely the problems something like this can cause. If they can't repair the ship in the next day, it's likely to get towed out of its current berth to prevent any more delays.'

'So, what will you do in the meantime?'

'Jen and Jon—the chief purser—will make an announcement to all guests. It means we'll be docked here overnight. It also means we won't give guests a return time today, which is unusual. But that means that anyone who wants to can spend the night in Rome. Hopefully we'll have news that says we can set sail tomorrow afternoon at the latest and can try to negotiate with a few other ports.'

'What happens if you can't?'

Vittorio stood up and opened a giant wardrobe, pulling out some clothes. 'It gets complicated. Cruise companies can sue each other around ruined schedules. Because it happens so infrequently, that generally doesn't happen. Passengers can get upset when the schedule changes, so we'll see how the mood is today. Usually, if they know it's no fault of our own, chances are they'll take it in good spirits. Jen might organise some night-time activity for some passengers who are interested.'

Sydney crossed her legs and smiled at him. 'I've heard the Trevi Fountain is beautiful at night.' She gestured with her hands. 'All lit up against a dark sky.'

He gave her an appreciative nod. 'You're right. And Jen is probably already on that. But—' he moved closer, pulling her up towards him '—if you'd like to have dinner in Rome tonight, and visit the Trevi Fountain, we can do that.'

She looked down at her sheet. 'I'll need to get dressed first.'

He sighed. 'Pity.'

She kissed him on the cheek. 'I can't wait to explore today. Sort out what you need to, then come and find me when you're ready to go.' She picked up her dress from the floor. 'I, in the meantime, will try to retrieve the rest of my clothes.'

Her brother rang her as she exited the shower. 'What?'

There was a pause at the end of the line. 'Eh, you're making some internet headlines.'

She blinked. 'What?'

'If you search *Is the love boat really successful?* you'll see what I mean.'

She paused and pulled out her tablet. It only

took a few scrolls to see the full effects. There were a series of photos of her and Vittorio. It was virtually charting their romance, from a picture at the waterfalls, to the dinner date from the beginning, a shot of them sharing drinks, and the picture of the intended kiss at Pompeii. She skimmed the first article. 'It calls me an archaeologist,' she said, immediately annoyed.

Peter sighed. 'Have you read the rest?'

'Give me a minute.'

She scrolled further and stopped at a picture of Vittorio with a supermodel on his arm. Alona. Thank goodness he'd warned her. Alona was one of those people who went by one name—she was *that* famous. She was stunning—tall, blonde, and extremely thin. Sydney's skin prickled as she read what followed.

'Oh,' she sighed.

'Oh?' said Peter. 'Is that all I'm going to get? Do you know what you're getting into?'

She shook her head, even though he wasn't there to see it. 'Actually, I do. Vittorio told me about this, and what she'd implied about him. She doesn't actually say that he was controlling or coercive if you read her actual quotes. It's just how the press interpreted things.'

'It's how the world interpreted it,' her brother cut in. 'Should I be worried?'

She thought about brushing him off, but Sydney had never lied to her brother before, and at the age of twenty-nine, she didn't want to start.

'No, you shouldn't be worried—because I'm not worried. I guess you could say that we're dating. He seems nice. I like him.'

'You like him?' His words dripped with sarcasm. 'Sydney, you say that about virtually no one.'

She smiled. 'Damn. I thought I was being subtle and low-key.'

Peter sighed. 'Jess is worried too. Promise me this is all a storm in a teacup.'

A tear brimmed in her eye, and she could sense in the silence that followed he'd realised he'd used another of their mother's favourite sayings.

'I miss her,' she whispered, letting that tear fall down her cheek.

Peter stayed silent for a few moments longer. 'I miss her too. But you haven't really given yourself any time to mourn her. To say goodbye.'

'I had work. I had deadlines,' she said quickly.

'Josef would've understood,' he cut her off equally quickly. 'You left two hours after the funeral, Syd. I had to pack up part of the house myself, and her clothes. Have you any idea how hard that was?'

She was shaking now, because she *did* understand, which was why she'd had to get herself away from it. And she was completely aware that Peter knew that too.

'You have to come back to the house sometime,' he sighed. 'She left it to us both, and you know I don't need it. Jess and I are settled.'

But that was just the thing. The thought of walking back through those doors and knowing her mother wouldn't be there—the smell of her perfume, or her preferred house polish—it would all just open up the gaping hole that was sitting in the middle of her chest.

'I will.' Her voice shook as she said the words, because she didn't really mean them.

'You won't.' His voice was more determined than hers. 'You have to come back. There are some things she wanted you to keep. Once this holiday is over, you should come home.'

The silence started to envelop her. 'It's not home anymore,' she finally said.

He paused, then agreed. 'I know it's not. Not without her. But maybe we sell the house, and you can find a place to buy yourself, to create new memories.'

'Maybe.' Her voice was quiet. She still wanted to avoid all this.

'Maybe,' he repeated in a resigned tone that told her he didn't really believe her.

Then he must have realised he still had an opportunity here.

'So, about this guy. You don't have a good track history for vetting guys. I feel like Jess and I should make you fill out some checklist before we agree to you dating him.'

She sighed, relieved he'd changed the subject, even if it was to Vittorio. 'You booked me on this cruise, so it's entirely your fault, both of you, that I met him. And just so you know, I had a great time at the waterfalls in Bosnia, a fabulous time at Pompeii yesterday, and will likely have an even better time in Rome, today and tonight.' Then she added, just for wickedness, 'I did nearly get killed in Santorini right enough, but hey, I'm still here.'

'What? What do you mean you nearly got killed in Santorini?' he exclaimed.

'Stampeding donkeys. Think it might be an occupational hazard there. Got to go, say hello to Jess for me.' She hung up, still smiling, knowing that he'd spend the next ten minutes searching the internet to see exactly what she meant.

But his words stuck with her. She'd been in the same place since her mother died. Not really ready to move on. And that didn't just apply to grieving; it applied to her whole life. Here she was, excited about meeting someone. But was she really ready to think about anything else—to think about a potential relationship with Vittorio—when she knew her head and heart still had unfinished business elsewhere?

She didn't like to admit it. But until she took the final steps to grieve for her mother, sell the house, and pack up the rest of the contents, she really wouldn't be able to commit to moving on and forming new relationships.

She wanted to keep pretending that part of her life didn't exist—because then she didn't need to deal with it. Then she could pretend Egypt was her everything, and all the painful parts of her life could continue to be ignored. But was she really doing herself any favours? And if the feelings she currently had towards Vittorio continued to build—what would she do then?

For now, she had Rome. A place that was an archaeologist's dream, and she also had the perfect host. Maybe she could push things away for another day.

Dressing for Rome was easy, she picked a long-patterned skirt, flat shoes, a red shirt, and her hat and sunglasses. This time she had to wait a little longer for Vittorio, but she knew he was sorting out important things so it didn't bother her. The announcements about the change to the itinerary had been made, and most passengers seemed good natured about it.

It only took her a few moments of observation to realise that most people's reason to come on this cruise was about being on the love boat, and looking to find a partner. The port stops were nice, but not the priority.

She could see couples chatting together, some mild flirtation, a few holding hands. Something sparked inside her brain. She'd treated ending up here as something bad—maybe even as an insult. But others had genuinely come here for this. They wanted to meet someone. They wanted to have fun. They wanted to find love. And she had. Without even trying.

Her skin prickled. Had she just even had that thought? No, no way. You couldn't possibly find love in a few days. Yes, she'd found someone that she was very attracted to, who made her feel connected, and who certainly knew how to keep her happy in the bedroom. But did that equate to love?

She was momentarily annoyed with herself for letting her brain even move in that direction, when Vittorio ran down the steps towards her and dropped a kiss on her cheek. 'Ready for a fabulous day in Rome?'

And every other thought was pushed away. Because yes, she was ready for this, and wanted to enjoy every second.

The weather was hot, but the pre-bought tickets meant they could skip the queue at the Colosseum. The pink-and-red limestone amphitheatre seemed to rise out of the ground as they turned a corner towards it.

Sydney let out a small squeak as it came into view, her smile wide and her hand on her chest. 'I always think it looks like aliens came and sat it down there,' she admitted, starting to laugh.

He opened his mouth to reply but she held up her hand. 'Don't worry, I definitely think that about the pyramids too.' She pressed her nose up against the window, and then changed her mind and buzzed it down, letting the wind blow through her hair. 'It always makes me wonder how they managed to build something so spectacular, all those years ago. Fifty thousand people—that's how many it used to hold. Can you imagine what Rome must have been like in those days?'

Vittorio sat back and let her talk. It was the passion in her voice. The wonder in her eyes as she looked at something she loved. He'd never met someone like her. He loved that she loved her job. He loved that she was sharing that passion with him. He'd always been proud of his Italian heritage, and the fact that he got to bring her here today just made it all the better.

He was still questioning what had happened last night. Of course, he'd wanted it to happen. But they'd crossed a line now. A line he'd been happy to cross. But what might it mean?

They joined the much shorter queue and left the option of the guided tour behind, wanting to explore on their own.

'Wait,' she said as they climbed the stairs, then held her hand out to Vittorio.

'What is it?'

'I want to close my eyes,' she admitted. 'My favourite thing here is that first sight of the pure majesty of the place when you're standing on the upper floor.'

He smiled and took her hand. 'Don't worry, you can trust me.'

He led her over to the edge and positioned her to get the best view of the whole building, the seats beneath them and the arena floor.

He stood behind her, hands on her hips and whispered in her ear. 'Okay, ready, in three, two, one.'

He felt her suck in her breath in that moment and sensed the wonder as they looked out at what stretched in front of them.

Vittorio was sure he had the exact same sensation. The scale of the place was almost overwhelming. Knowing the history made it verge on terrifying. The difference in the seating and the class system that had been in place dictating where people sat. The sense of dread that must have been present in every gladiator's gut. The blood thirst, from fifty thousand people screaming, willing someone to die. The noise must have been phenomenal.

He didn't say those words out loud and didn't need to. Because he could see it in her face as she took her time, her eyes sweeping the auditorium and clearly contemplating everything that he was.

He pulled out his camera and moved her closer to him, snapping a picture with them both, showing the Colosseum in the background.

They stayed there for a while. Watching the rest of the tourists and drinking in the atmosphere of the place. He didn't want to rush her out of somewhere she clearly loved visiting. Finally, she gave a sigh and pointed at the arena floor. 'Let's go down to the gladiator gate and join that tour.'

He gave a nod, and they made their way down, moving through the ancient gate—also known at the Gate of Death—where gladiators and animals entered the arena for sometimes their final battle. Seeing the Colosseum from the reconstructed arena floor and the position of the gladiators gave a totally new perspective.

'How intimidating must this have been?' breathed Sydney, looking upwards. 'All these people staring down at you, shouting, wanting you dead.'

They moved down to the hypogeum, the vast

network of tunnels and chambers that served as the back stage for the Colosseum. Here, the gladiators, animals and machinery were all stored. A range of pulleys and winches were devised to propel the gladiators or animals up into the arena via trapdoors.

It was dark, damp, imposing, and still had a strange ancient odour about the place.

Vittorio shuddered and Sydney turned and put her hands flat on his chest. 'I have loved every second, but I think it's time for us to get back up into Rome's sunshine.'

'I agree,' he said, taking her hand and leading her back outside. It was never quiet outside the Colosseum, and it took them a few moments to find their car again.

'Where to?'

She counted off on her fingers. 'Palatine Hill, Roman Forum and Circus Maximus.'

He sat back in his seat. 'All of them?'

'Absolutely. We can do St Peter's later in the day when hopefully it's not so busy.'

'And the Trevi Fountain tonight?'

Her eyes gleamed as she smiled at him. 'That would be fantastic. I've only ever seen it during the day. I'd love to see it at night.'

Vittorio signalled to his driver to take them to everywhere she wanted to go. He also managed to fit in a visit to Mercato Trionfale, the biggest food market in Rome, with a dazzling array of stalls, where they picked up some food for the day.

Sydney didn't stop talking or asking questions. They posed for pictures all across the city, people watching and picking up coffee or gelato as the inspiration struck them.

By the time they made it to St Peter's Basilica, both of them were starting to wilt. 'You're sure you don't want to visit the Vatican and the Sistine Chapel?'

She shook her head. 'I've done that before, and my favourite part was definitely St Peter's. I felt rushed the last time because we didn't have much time to spend there.'

He gave a nod, and they walked across St Peter's Square towards the imposing white-domed building. Entry was free but they had to go through a security check, and once that was complete, they entered the large building.

The first obvious thing to strike them both was how noise flowed through the building. With the large dome, noise seemed to amplify, and even though most people were whispering in the building, it was amazing how a single voice could carry.

Sydney held his hand, walking slowly, smiling at a group of nuns praying at one altar, and watching a queue of people waiting for confession.

'Have you ever done that?' she whispered in Vittorio's ear.

'Of course.' He gave her a mock-shocked look. 'I was brought up a good Roman Catholic boy.'

She sighed. 'I wasn't, and I've always been kind of curious about it all.'

'You want to join a queue?'

She shook her head. 'I'd never disrespect someone's religion, but I think I'd like to see the inside of a confessional box.'

He wagged his finger at her. 'You have to fully convert to see the inside of a confessional booth.'

She sighed again and put her hand into his. 'You win. Let's look around.'

There were over one hundred tombs in St Peter's, and it would really have taken days to spend the time to do them justice. There were also multiple clocks, works of art, sculptures, and a whole variety of niches containing statues of some of the saints.

People treated the place with the reverence and respect it was due. There were several staff on duty who were happy to answer questions about the items on display or the history of the building.

As they moved around the large space, he was conscious of Sydney's every move. She was interested and curious as well as respectful. It didn't take him long to realise how much he was enjoying spending time in her company. When he'd made the suggestion that they team up, it had seemed like a mutual convenience. Neither of them would have to continue to take part in the love boat activities, and both of them could keep themselves happy.

But things had changed rapidly. Sydney Scott was fun, and interesting, and one hell of a hot Egyptologist.

All things he probably shouldn't think, and definitely shouldn't say out loud.

But they'd already gone past that point. Last night had taken this relationship up a notch. And the truth was, he didn't want that to stop.

He tried to put his finger on what it was about Sydney. He didn't think she'd told him everything about her that he needed to know. But he did think she'd been honest. He could trust her. At least it seemed like he could.

Yes, they were a million miles apart in geography, upbringing and career plans. There were currently no stars aligned on this planet that seemed to allow them to be together. But he wasn't worrying about that.

He was worrying about now. And if she would enjoy dinner tonight and the trip to the Trevi

Fountain. But his truth was, that he wanted to keep her happy. And he hadn't felt like that in…

He stopped and took a breath. Four years. He hadn't felt like that in four years.

The damage left behind by Alona was deeper than he'd thought.

Parts of his brain just didn't want to go there. Things were time limited between him and Sydney, and he didn't want to waste a minute.

When she finally stopped admiring the exhibits in St Peter's, she came and leaned against him. 'I think I'm finally done.'

He smiled. 'Then let's go, because Rome is the most romantic city in the world, and we're not finished here yet.'

As they climbed back into the car, Sydney knew she had to reach for something sweet and refreshing. She was flagging. The heat of the day, plus the length of time they'd been on their feet, meant if she could close her eyes right now, she would.

But their day wasn't done yet, and she didn't want it to be.

'Do you want to go back to the ship and change for dinner, or do you want to stay in the city?'

Sydney thought for a few moments. The journey to and from the ship in traffic could add time to their journey that would delay them. She looked down at what she was wearing and couldn't pretend that she didn't want to change.

'Is there anywhere nearby we could shop?'

He nodded and signalled to the driver to take them to a street filled with exclusive boutiques for both men and women. 'Take your pick,' he said.

She could have easily spent all day in these shops, looking, but not buying. 'Where are we going for dinner?' she asked, trying to judge what she should wear.

'It's a secret,' he said. 'But buy something nice.'

'That's it? That's the clue?'

'That's the clue.' He smiled as he walked into the nearest designer store.

It was almost like a challenge. So, Sydney accepted. She didn't usually spend much money on clothes mainly because she bought what she needed. And working in digs in Egypt meant she didn't have much call for nice.

But Vittorio, or his company, had already gifted her a beautiful dress on the ship, and Sydney was more than capable of spending whatever it took.

She moved into the nearest shop and looked through the rails. Lots of beautiful clothes, some in tiny sizes, but also lots of bland colours. One of the assistants came to speak to her in rapid Italian.

Sydney held up her hand. 'I'm so sorry, I don't speak Italian, but I'm looking for a dress.'

Without a blink the woman switched into perfect English. 'No problem. What do you like?'

Sydney looked around and pulled a regretful face. 'Something elegant, long…and with a bit of colour if you have it.'

The woman looked her up and down, 'Yes, jewel colours will suit you best. Let me check in the back.' She led Sydney through to one of the dressing rooms, handing her a glass of champagne. 'Wait here.'

Sydney looked at the glass in her hand and sat down in the velvet chair. She'd half expected to get the *Pretty Woman* treatment in a shop like this, and to have been looked down on. Instead, the sales assistant seemed completely at ease, and helpful.

She came back five minutes later with a few dresses. Navy sequin, purple, and a dark burgundy. She hung them up so Sydney could have a better look. 'What do you think of these?'

'Gorgeous,' answered Sydney automatically, because they all were. And they weren't tiny. They looked like normal-size dresses. It seemed the sales assistant had guessed her size just by looking.

And it wasn't just the size she'd guessed correctly. When Sydney tried the dresses on, she realised the cut of each dress favoured her figure. After much deliberating, and also choosing a selection of matching underwear, she settled on the navy dress with thin straps, a vee neck, and several collections of matching sequins in thick diagonal stripes across it that made her figure even more flattering.

'Thank you so much,' she said to the sales assistant as she added gold sandals to the purchase and didn't even blink at the final price.

Vittorio was waiting outside for her in a pair of well-cut trousers, dark shiny shoes, and a tailored shirt. 'Ready?' he asked, holding out his hand.

'Ready,' she agreed, taking in just how handsome he looked tonight.

As she slid into the car he whispered in her ear, 'You look stunning.'

The journey to the restaurant was short, but Vittorio led her up a set of winding stairs and out to a rooftop terrace. As soon as she stepped outside, she knew the night would be magical.

The air was warm. The sun starting to dip in the sky, sending streaks of orange, red and yellow across the sky, backdropping the Colosseum like the magnificent artefact that it was.

'What a perfect place for dinner,' she breathed, as the waiter pulled out her chair for her.

They feasted on marinated duck breast with sage-infused cream, and sweet Maritozzo bread with cream and candied orange peel. Both courses were paired with wine, and the tables around them featured couples talking quietly while admiring the yellow-lit arches in the Colosseum.

'It's breathtaking.' She smiled. 'Thank you for finding this place.'

He raised his glass to her. 'My pleasure. I wanted you to be able to see the best of Rome at night.' He gave her another smile. 'And, we're not finished yet.' He glanced under the table. 'Though I fear that those shoes might mean I need to carry you part of the way.'

'What do you mean?'

'You'll see.'

He led her back to the car and they moved through the dark streets of Rome, stopping near what looked like a small dark street.

As soon they left the car she understood. The streets here were old and contained the common Italian paving that resembled cobblestones. She held tightly on to Vittorio's arms as they moved slowly along the streets, exiting to the white lights of the Trevi Fountain.

It was quite late now, nearly eleven o'clock,

and the fountain was nowhere near as busy as it was during the day.

They had plenty of space to move around and admire the carved baroque fountain, with its figures, arches, and columns.

Sydney didn't touch the water that flowed into the shallow pool of the fountain, but she could see the many coins glistening in the moonlight.

'Come this way,' said Vittorio as he took her hand and led her slowly to the side.

'What's this?' she asked, staring at the much less grand small basin with two small spouts.

'It's the Fountain of Lovers,' he said in a low voice. 'Haven't you heard of it?'

She shook her head. The other few people who were around were all focused on the main fountain. No one else had followed them to this side.

'What does it mean?' she asked.

He pointed at the spouts. 'Couples who drink from the spouts are meant to be guaranteed lasting love,' he said simply.

She blinked, wondering if she'd heard him correctly.

'That sounds…important,' she managed.

'It would seem wasteful to be here and to not at least try to honour the legend and tradition,' he said in a playful tone.

Her eyes met his. 'How did this start?' she asked, her curious brain unable to stop her asking.

He looked serious. ‘The tradition started with soldiers and their fiancées coming here before they experienced wartime separations.’

‘Wow,’ she said, as the enormity of that hit home. Then she gave him a small smile. ‘In that case, it seems only respectful to carry on the tradition.’

She pulled her curls back and bent to drink from one of the spouts. When she lifted her chin, Vittorio did the same, and then met her in the middle with a kiss.

‘Are there any other Italian traditions you want to introduce me to?’ she whispered.

‘There is.’ He smiled as he took her hand again and led her back in front of the main fountain.

While they’d been at the Fountain of Lovers, several street musicians had set up in one of the nearby recesses. The music they started playing was classical, with a haunting but beautiful tone. Somehow it fitted the occasion perfectly.

‘Shall we dance?’ Vittorio asked.

Sydney tried to still her rapidly beating heart. If someone had asked her to imagine what her dream date might be, she could never even have guessed it’d be something as perfect as this had been.

She put her hands lightly on his shirt. ‘I’d love to.’

As they moved to the music, the cobbled stones beneath her feet were forgotten. All that was there was the movement of his body next to hers. The way his muscular frame blended perfectly against the curves of her body. The way his eyes never left her face.

The gentle touch of his hand at the bottom of her bare back. The scent of his woody aftershave. The tiny shadow around his jaw.

And when he bent his head and dropped some featherlight kisses on her shoulder, her skin flamed with pleasure and anticipation.

She was in the perfect place, with the perfect person.

And because of that, as the musicians kept playing, Sydney kept dancing, her head wondering about what might lie ahead.

CHAPTER EIGHT

THERE WAS A call from an unknown number on his mobile the next day when he woke up next to Sydney again. There was no message, which happened sometimes, so he ignored it.

Something had shifted for him. This was no casual convenience anymore. This was a full-on dating agreement that was leading to a place he hadn't been in a while. It could be that their lifestyles would be just too incompatible and at the end of the fortnight, they would just walk away from each other with positive memories. But Vittorio already sensed that wasn't something he was prepared to do.

He wanted more. But he needed to have the conversation with Sydney, to make sure she was on the same page. He thought she was, but he didn't actually know it.

The ship had sailed this morning from Rome, giving them an extra day at sea while they headed towards Monte Carlo.

Another one of his own cruise ships had adjusted its own schedule, adding in a bonus visit to Palerma in Sicily to allow the *Minerva* to dock a day late at Monaco.

If there were complaints later, the company would deal with them appropriately.

Jen was in overdrive, juggling to organise a day's activities at sea. But the crew were adaptable, adding in extra shows, events, and physical activities for passengers.

Sydney was delighted, as now she could have afternoon tea with Mary and Jim, and Vittorio had made sure it was scheduled at their finest restaurant. 'I'll try to join you if I can,' he'd said as he left her lying on his bed and made his way to the office.

Jen approached him with a smile. 'Vittorio, we need to chat.'

'What is it?'

She leaned her hand on the desk and gave him a careful smile. 'It seems that you and Sydney are one of our headline acts.'

'What do you mean?'

'It means that your *romance*—' she emphasised the word '—is taking social media by storm.'

He groaned, wondering if he should admit that what started as a fake dating arrangement had turned into something more. He really didn't want to be under the spotlight.

'I don't want to take part.'

Jen sat down in front of him. 'Vittorio, this is exactly what we want. People talking about the *Minerva* cruise. People saying that the matchmaking exercises have worked. These headlines are good headlines, and we should use them to our advantage. We have a small window here. If you and Sydney agree to be photographed again, then they will be able to use that with the rest of the pictures.'

Vittorio put his head in his hands. 'I don't see how the chief executive being part of a dating game can ever play out in my favour.'

'And that's just the point.' He now believed that Jen had prepared for this chat and would have an answer to anything that he brought up. 'It humanises you. Up until now you've just been a mysterious figurehead for the company. Now you're a man that—like other people in the world—has taken a chance on love.'

He shook his head. 'No. That makes me look a bit pathetic.'

'Not if we spin it the way we want. You don't think you're too good for the services we offer on our cruises. You are happy to take a chance the way other people do.' She raised her eyebrows. 'Hashtag MinervaLoveBoat is trending.'

It struck a nerve. If he hadn't taken part, he would never have met Sydney. And he was grateful to have met her.

Of course, he could pretend that fate hadn't played a hand here and brought them to this place at the same time. But even if they had ended up on the same ship, if the matchmaking agenda hadn't been in place, they would likely have never crossed paths.

That actually made him a bit wary. He hated that chance had played a big factor here, and that by some other roll of the die, they might never have met.

But surely that must be the same for lots of couples around the world?

He gave an enormous sigh. This could all go horribly wrong. 'Okay, but let me check again with Sydney first. I need to make sure she's comfortable now that you're telling me we're trending.'

'As you wish.' Jen nodded.

The day had been very relaxed. Although there were a hundred activities on board that Sydney could have taken part in, she was more than happy to relax in her cabin, spend time in her hot tub staring out at the ocean, and then visiting the library on board the ship.

She was lucky when she entered, as she was the only person there. The carved light wood bookshelves were densely packed, and there was even a rolling ladder attached to the shelves. She took a few moments wheeling it back and forward, wondering if she could fit something like this into her mother's house.

But that stopped her. Because something like this wouldn't suit the cottage-style bungalow her mother and father had shared. They'd described parts of it as quirky. But that was because the walls weren't straight and the floors were uneven.

The kitchen fitters had experienced a nightmare ten years ago when trying to install a new kitchen, with no cabinets lining up straight and lots of adjustments having to be made.

The rooms were small and although as a child it had been a wonderful place to be brought up, complete with wide gardens and a stream running along the edge of their property, as a teenager and then an adult, both Sydney and her brother knew that the work needed on the cottage would far outweigh any price they could achieve.

It really had to be sold. This was mainly what she'd been avoiding for the last eighteen months. Once the bungalow was gone, it was gone. There was no chance to go back and breathe in the scent, sit on the slightly lumpy sofa and look out the small windows to the view outside.

She needed to actually do something about it. Her parents' estate was still paying the utility bills at the house, and while that wasn't a problem, it was never good leaving a property empty. It was difficult to insure an empty house.

She ran her fingers along the wood, liking the feel. It was wood, but it felt warm, as if it actually exuded some heat and was inviting you in.

Her eyes went to the books. There was a huge range, popular fiction including recent titles in romance, crime, historical, thrillers, sci-fi and fantasy. There was an equally large nonfiction section, lots of which covered ocean- and ship-related information, geography, climate, then moved onto all the celebrity memoirs and finally a section for children and teenagers.

She lifted up a book about an archaeologist she didn't know much about, a book about the Terracotta Army she hadn't seen before, and then finally settled on a crime thriller.

She opened the first one and before she knew it, she had to rush to get changed and join Mary and Jim for afternoon tea. They had already arrived and were talking to a woman, who gave Sydney a nod and moved off.

'Did she want to join us?' Sydney asked as she slid into a seat.

Mary shook her head and laughed. 'Jim and I have turned into the *Minerva*'s agony aunts.' There were crinkles around her eyes. 'We haven't been so entertained in years.'

At that point Sydney felt a hand on her back. Mary's eyes gleamed as Vittorio's rich accent filled the air. 'Would you mind if I joined you all?'

Jim nodded to the chair next to Sydney. 'You're the boss. We can't exactly throw you overboard.'

Vittorio gave a nod, still smiling as he sat down. 'Forgive me for overhearing, but you said you're now the ship's agony aunts? What does that mean?'

Sydney patted his hand. 'It's a very British expression. An agony aunt is someone who gives advice on problems. When I was young you could write into newspapers or magazines. Nowadays it's mainly online, or some TV shows have agony aunts to offer advice.'

Vittorio gave a nod as he settled his napkin on his lap. 'So, Mary, you've taken over this job on board?' He looked amused.

Mary beamed, saying, 'Oh, we have, and it's not just me. Jim too.'

Jim nodded, looking serious. 'Women *and* men,' he added. 'We're hearing all the stories.'

'So, people just come up and tell you their troubles?' asked Sydney.

'Relationship troubles.' Mary nodded. 'Trying to find a good match is a serious business. People have paid good money to come on this cruise. They don't want to waste their time with someone who isn't right for them.'

There it was again—how seriously people took this. Sydney was amazed, and a little embarrassed by her initial thoughts when she'd arrived.

She exchanged a glance with Vittorio and knew he was thinking the same thing.

The waiter came and took their order for tea or coffee, checked allergies, like and dislikes, and the food arrived in its tower, very quickly. The *Minerva* afternoon tea followed the traditional rules: An array of beautifully filled sandwiches alongside some sausage rolls and a tiny bowl of soup. The second tier was filled with a range of scones, clotted cream, and flavoured jams. The final tier had magnificent tiny cakes, mousses, and tray bakes.

Sydney's eyes swept up and down the tiers. 'There's no way we can eat all this.'

'I'll have a good go,' said Jim, already lifting his small plate.

Vittorio smiled in good humour. 'Me too.' She could tell he was pleased with the display, and that they were all so enamoured by it.

Sydney smiled and let the couple fill their plates while sipping at her soup. 'So, what happened that you had to delay your original cruise?' she asked.

They exchanged glances. 'I had to go for a biopsy,' said Jim in a firm voice.

The word gave a little shot of fear into Sydney's heart as Jim continued.

'The results weren't good, so we decided we didn't want to wait for treatment, we wanted to get out and enjoy ourselves.'

Sydney's throat was immediately dry. Under the table, Vittorio put a reassuring hand on her thigh. 'You're not getting treatment?' she asked, seeing the wetness in Mary's eyes.

The couple clasped hands for a moment. Jim shook his head. 'Not for me. The regime would be hard and won't cure me, only give me some more time.'

'Surely you want more time?' Sydney couldn't help the question. She could sense Vittorio tense next to her.

He gave a sad smile. 'Of course I do. But I want quality time. Not time wasting away and feeling terrible. I've seen it happen to too many of our friends. Months of debilitating treatment, with no assured outcome and their quality of life fading away.' He held out his hands, gesturing to the beautiful room they were in, with the white linen covered tables, and view of the ocean all around. 'This is what I want.'

'There weren't any other forms of treatment?'

Vittorio asked. 'Ones that wouldn't be so difficult?'

Mary shook her head, and it was clear she trying to keep herself together. 'Nothing proven.'

Sydney bit her lip. 'I understand,' she said. Because she did. Her mother had suffered from a similar disease.

After a gentle pause, Mary spoke as she squeezed Jim's hand. 'So, most of the advice we have been giving people has been about living for the moment, making decisions, and not wasting time.'

Something tingled inside Sydney. She knew these were exactly the kind of sentiments her mother would have shared. Vittorio took a deep breath next to her. 'I think you are both very brave. And I'm glad that you're here. If you need anything at all, just let me know. Nothing will be too much trouble. I mean it.'

Mary and Jim both gave appreciative nods.

'You should have set up charges for your counselling services,' said Sydney lightly.

'Oh no,' said Mary in a shocked voice. 'It's just surprising that so many people today don't have families around them like we do. They don't have places to go to for advice.'

Sydney gave a slow nod. 'I'm lucky, I have a brother and had good parents. But some families are toxic. And for others, found family is much better than the ones they are related too.' She looked at them both. A devoted couple, clearly ready for the next stage of their journey. 'Do you think you've helped some people find the magic that you have?'

Mary leaned back and sipped her tea. 'We hope so.'

Sydney could feel tears prickle her eyes but pushed them backwards. This wasn't the time or the place. Mary and Jim had made their choices, and they wanted to live life to the full. It should be celebrated.

She let herself try to relax. The afternoon tea was delicious, and the staff attentive. There was nothing to be faulted here. She was sitting on a beautiful cruise ship, with people that she valued.

But her minded drifted to Vittorio and the wonderful night they'd had. It was like someone had tried to find a perfect date and just dropped it into her lap.

'What are you smiling about?' Jim nudged her.

She shot a look at Vittorio, wondering how he would feel about her revealing a part of themselves. As his hand squeezed her thigh again, she knew he would be okay. After all, Jim and Mary had just shared privileged information with them.

'We were dancing last night at the Trevi Fountain,' she admitted.

'You two? Together?' Mary asked excitedly.

She nodded and put her hand on Vittorio's, raising them both to the table so Jim and Mary could see that they were entwined.

Mary gave them both an interested look. 'You were together in Santorini, and now in Rome?'

'In Dubrovnik and Pompeii too.'

Mary clapped her hands together. 'Another pair for our success list. How many is that now, Jim?'

'Twenty-two couples,' he said immediately, proving that his brain was still sharp.

'I think they should do this thing more often,' said Mary.

Vittorio leaned forward at the comment. 'You do? Why?'

'Because this is what life is about, isn't it? We all want companionship. But you should open it up to people our age. Lots of pensioners are on their own. They want company. It's hard to lose a partner at our age.' She gave Jim a little nod and straightened up. 'And for other couples too—whatever your age or sexuality—it can be hard out there to meet someone.'

Vittorio nodded in approval. 'I've just been in a company meeting about expanding the service.' He smiled at Sydney. 'After all, things do seem to be going well.'

For the next hour, they debated the pros and

cons of the matchmaking scheme, but by then it was clear that both Mary and Jim were tiring, and they made their excuses to return to their room.

As they stood to leave, Mary smiled at Sydney. 'You should send your brother a bottle of champagne to thank him for booking you on this cruise. Look how well things have worked out for you.' And then she bent and whispered in her ear as Jim shook hands with Vittorio, 'Find a way to make this work. Ask yourself what you want out of life.'

A warm feeling spread through her stomach as both Jim and Mary left. They were devoted to each other. She hated to imagine what the future might hold for them now.

Vittorio slid his arm around her shoulders and dropped a kiss on her cheek. 'I'll make sure our medical team keeps an eye on them.'

'I know you will,' she said sadly. 'They are so nice. They just don't deserve this.'

He nodded. 'But we have to respect them, and their decisions.'

She rested her head on his shoulder as she swallowed the lump in her throat. 'I know.'

Vittorio waited a few moments and gave her a nudge. 'Hey,' he said in a more jovial tone, clearly trying to lift the mood. 'What have you done about your brother?'

'Well, I have to admit he got a few angry texts the first few days. I was ready to never speak to him again.'

'He clearly had your best interests at heart.'

Sydney gave a slow nod. 'But how could he possibly know things would work out? He didn't know you and I would hit it off. You weren't even supposed to be on this ship. We have very different lives.'

Vittorio stiffened a little. 'Are you saying you have regrets?'

She shook her head immediately but bit her lip. 'I'm just saying I've had a wonderful few days together and wonder how this could work in future. Living in different countries isn't ideal.' Then she considered what really mattered. Mary's comment was making her think. What did she want? 'I've been let down quite a few times before. Trust isn't easy for me.'

'Or me,' said Vittorio quickly. 'It's not easy seeing things printed about you that aren't true.'

Sydney nodded, wondering how she would have felt in that position. She reached up and touched the button on the front of his shirt. 'I like where we are just now,' she admitted.

'So do I,' he admitted then took a breath. 'So, why don't we try some brutal honesty. What do you want in the immediate future—or in the next five years?'

Sydney felt her stomach clench. No one had ever asked her this question. And her immediate response felt quite primal.

'I want to have my own dig,' was the first thing that came out of her mouth, because that had been her ambition since she was a teenager.

She saw a flash of something in his eyes and wondered if she'd disappointed him. Had he wanted her to say she wanted a husband, and a family? Her stomach remained in a clench. Maybe she'd misjudged things, but she couldn't honestly say that right now, because she knew deep down she had to deal with other things first.

'And?'

The word was left hanging. Maybe now was the time for honesty. Maybe if she was honest, he would walk away like men in her past had done. She didn't think she'd done anything deliberately to drive them away, but part of her always wondered if the next man would abandon her too. Would it make things easier if she just found out now, spoiling the magic bubble she found herself in?

Sydney took a deep breath. 'And… I have things to deal with back in England. Things that have been waiting for a while.' She sighed, 'I need to sort out my mother's old house. It needs to be sold, but I can't stand the thought of emptying it.'

Vittorio closed his hand over Sydney's. 'You've hinted at things but haven't really told me the story. When did your mother die?'

She bit her lip as tears automatically filled in her eyes. 'Just over eighteen months ago.'

'It was a surprise?'

She shook her head. 'Yes, and no.'

'What does that mean?' His tone was sympathetic.

'She had a long-standing cancer diagnosis but had managed it well. She had nurses who visited her at home for as long as she was able to stay there. We always knew it would shorten her life expectancy, but she had a bad chest infection, went into hospital, and never came back out. It all happened so quickly.'

She hated saying these words out loud, because all the old pent-up feelings were threatening to spill over.

Vittorio was very calm, his voice soothing. 'I can imagine how horrible that was for you. And the house? Hasn't Peter offered to help with that?'

She sighed. 'He has. He wants to get it done. In a way I wish we didn't have to sell it. I'd love to be in a position to let one of the cancer charities use it as a family getaway, for families that need a break when dealing with cancer. They helped us so much when Mum was sick. It's a lovely cottage in the country with a stream at the bottom of the garden. A place where people could try to forget for a while.' She shook her head for a second. 'But, unfortunately, I'm not a millionaire, so it's only a pipe dream. The reality is I'm going to need to do something different to move on.'

'And how do you want to move on?' he asked gently.

'I'd like to buy someplace new. Not sure where yet,' she admitted.

'Someplace you can make a fresh start?'

'Yes,' she let out on a breath.

'Is there anything else you could see in your future?' The little sparkle had returned to his eyes, and she knew she could give him a truthful answer, one that he would like.

Sydney licked her lips. 'I'd like to keep seeing someone I'm involved with,' she said, letting a smile come back to her face. 'I'd like to see where things might go.'

He gave her the biggest grin and held out his hand to her. 'Then why don't we go explore Monaco tomorrow, and start finding out.'

CHAPTER NINE

MONTE CARLO, AND MORE importantly Port Hercules in Monaco, was one of the most popular cruise ship stops.

From the buzz on the ship this morning, it seemed that just about everyone wanted to disembark.

There was another missed call on his phone from an unknown number with no message. But it was a different number than the one before, so he just wrote it off as someone dialling incorrectly.

There were also some messages from Jen telling him to check social media. The *Minerva* was starting to make worldwide headlines. They appeared to be trending on all social media channels and the influencer's on-board streaming content had exploded. All good news that he could consider later, because right now, he had too much going on.

Monaco had soared into view with its gorgeous coastline and glittering array of white luxury yachts all bobbing in crystal-blue waters as if they were just asking people to photograph them.

Vittorio recognised a few of them. Some from people he liked, and some from people he would prefer not eat dinner alongside. That was the danger of the beautiful resorts. People could pop up at any time.

At least it wasn't Grand Prix time. Monaco was always crammed to the brim with celebrities, their entourages, and visiting dignitaries at that time. Most of the cruises didn't like coinciding with the Grand Prix as often their passengers couldn't view the city in any meaningful way.

As he waited the few minutes for Sydney to appear, he had a little pit of dread in his stomach. There weren't any real significant archaeological artefacts to see in Monte Carlo. They planned on just visiting the normal tourist spots and having a relaxing day. But something about the schedule pinned on his office wall made him feel as if he were on a countdown.

Sydney appeared in a flowing black skirt and red top, sunglasses on her head and a black bag slung over her shoulder. 'Ready to hit the high spots?' she asked.

His heart lifted just at the sight of her and the sound of her voice. He was getting used to this. He was getting used to seeing Sydney every day, being around her, waking up with her in his bed. The realisation was startling.

But something deep in his gut was now uncomfortable. He was being untrue, to himself, and to Sydney. He always kept his heart buttoned up, but now it wasn't buttoned up anymore; she'd practically burst it wide open. They'd started this relationship as a lie. A pretence. They'd agreed to fake date. It wasn't like that anymore, and though they'd chatted and skirted around the edges of what they both might want in the future, had they actually said things out loud?

He hadn't told her that he loved her. But he knew that, was sure of it. But she'd told him she'd been burned before, and he didn't want anything to push her away. Maybe she was still happy in the bubble of pretend?

What if, after the cruise ended and they went back to their normal lives, she changed her mind?

He pushed those thoughts away. He could deal with all that later. Right now was for showing Sydney the parts of Monte Carlo she'd never seen before. They could continue their little bubble a while longer—surely?

As soon as they set foot in the central square, Sydney glanced at the outside tables at the coffee shop opposite the casino and said, 'Let's relax for a bit.'

They sat at a table, ordering coffee at a ridiculous price and watching the Monte Carlo world go by.

'This is fascinating,' whispered Sydney as she watched a thin elderly woman dressed in an exquisite cream wool suit and high heels teeter towards them, sitting at a table and pulling a Chihuahua from her bag.

The dog proceeded to yap at anyone who dared walk past, but the staff seemed to know her, and immediately brought her a black coffee and some water for her dog.

Another two women appeared, dressed in spectacular flowing, bright kaftans. They sat at another table, throwing the occasional scowl at the older woman, who ignored them completely.

A man with a shock of white hair—nearly all standing on end, an exquisite suit, a very wobbly walking stick—and an extremely good-looking, much younger woman sat at another table. He promptly fell asleep while she talked on her phone to everyone she knew and admired her own jewellery.

'It's like a whole other world,' breathed Sydney, fascinated too by the people walking up and down the steps of the casino.

'It's like a soap opera,' said Vittorio, shaking his head, but equally happy to sit with her and people watch.

A few moments later, a famous race car driver strode past them with a newspaper in hand.

'This place just gets more interesting by the minute,' Sydney laughed.

'Wine?' Vittorio suggested.

'Oh, absolutely!' she agreed.

They sat for another hour, sipping wine and watching the rest of the world go by. The older lady finally left, but not before her Chihuahua cocked its leg and peed on some other woman's leg, who screamed and caused a scene.

'Do you want to visit the casino?' Vittorio asked.

She shook her head. 'Let's do the palace tour, and visit the Grace Kelly rose garden.' She gave him a wink. 'Then I wouldn't mind a little drive through the tunnel, just to see what it's like.'

He laughed. 'I think we can arrange that.'

The day was absolutely more chilled than any they had spent together. Monaco was small, things were close together, which helped, but the most important thing for Vittorio was just having the chance to be around one another.

Sydney was still Sydney, asking a hundred questions on the tour of the palace, and wandering around the rose garden in the afternoon sun as if it were the most important place on the planet to her. She liked to give things her full attention, and he loved that about her.

They climbed into a local taxi and asked the driver to take them around part of the famous Grand Prix track. The driver had obviously done this many times before and regaled them with tales of what he knew, all those who had crashed and some of the superstitions around the race-track.

He deliberately sped up as they moved through the tunnel, and Sydney gave a little gasp, leaning up against Vittorio as they rounded the corner. 'It's really tight,' she whispered. 'I mean, I knew it was, I just didn't expect it to be…that tight.'

He smiled at her and wrapped an arm around her shoulders. 'Had enough excitement for the day?'

Her hand moved over to the front of his chest. 'There's been something so nice about this. I can't remember the last time I really relaxed, or people watched.'

'Me either,' he admitted. 'Maybe we both need to slow down a bit.'

He watched her face contort a little, and then tried to pretend that it didn't.

'What?' he asked.

She wrinkled her nose. 'Slowing down.' She paused for a moment. 'It sounds good in theory.'

'But?'

'But what if I miss something? Like a new discovery? Something I've worked on for years.'

'Discoveries get made all over the world, every day. You can't be at all of them.'

She slapped her hand loosely on his thigh. 'I know that. But I mean in Egypt. What if I slow down, and then miss one of the biggest discoveries in Egyptian history?'

'You don't think those have already happened?'

She pulled another face. 'Well, yes, and no. You just never know what else might be out there.'

'What's been your best discovery so far?'

'The best thing I've found is a city.'

She smiled at his stunned expression.

'I was part of a dig in 2021 that discovered the Lost Golden City of Aten, near Luxor. It's the largest ancient city ever found, and dates back to the reign of Amenhotep III.'

He looked at her in awe. She really was a wonderful woman. And for a moment all he could focus on was how much he admired her. It took him a few seconds to get back to the point of their chat.

'But if there was a new discovery, couldn't you just go back and take part in it?'

'Yeah. Me and the rest of the world.' She gave him a rueful smile. 'You have no idea how ruthless the world of archaeology is. Even if it was my dig, every internationally published archaeologist in the world would make their case to get on-site.'

Vittorio took a deep breath. 'I love that you love what you do. I love that you have passion for your job. But are you going to spend your whole life terrified that you might miss out?'

Sydney bit her lip. Someone else had sat her down and had this conversation with her. Asking her what she wanted out of life. It seemed like all the planets were aligning somewhere with Sydney at their centre. Demanding that she take the time to ask herself the hard questions.

She put her hand on her heart. 'I think, honestly, I will always be terrified that I will miss out. But I know I can't be on every dig in Egypt, let alone in the rest of the world. Trying to think rationally about something you love is hard.'

The words hovered on his lips, and he wondered if he should actually say them. Things were teetering between them. His feelings grew every day, but had he misread this situation, and was he about to make a fool of himself?

'Aren't there other things to love too?'

Silence.

The car had pulled up outside an exclusive restaurant, but Vittorio wasn't sure this was a conversation to have in public.

Sydney looked up at him, tears brimming in her eyes. 'What do you mean?'

He still didn't know if he should say this. His heart missed a few beats. 'I mean…what about us?'

She blinked, and he knew she was searching for words. His stomach gave a few rolls. This was the part when she said, *Well, I've enjoyed myself, but I'm not looking for anything serious.*

'What about us?' she repeated instead. Then, when he thought she wasn't going to continue, she gave a little smile. 'Do you want there to be an us?'

It was the tiny hopeful inclination in her voice that almost tipped him. He put his hands on her upper arms, turning her so she was fully facing him in the car. 'Of course, I do.'

The edges of her lips turned upwards again. 'But—'

He knew she was going to ask a whole host of questions—like how would they make this work, how often would they see each other—all perfectly rational questions that he didn't have the answers to right now, so he silenced her with a kiss.

'I didn't expect to feel like this,' he said as his kisses moved from her lips to her neck.

'Me either,' she answered breathlessly.

After a few moments she pulled back and looked him in the eye. 'Vittorio, promise me that I can trust you. I'm not in this to get my heart broken again.'

'You can trust me,' he answered immediately. 'I won't break that trust.'

He saw her take in a kind of shuddery breath. This was big for her. Just like it was for him.

He bent his head to her ear. 'If you'd told me this time a few weeks ago that I would meet someone on the love cruise, I would have bet the whole company on it not being true.'

She smiled at him. 'Just as well you didn't.' She ran her fingers down the side of his face. 'But you might as well know, I've now lost a bet with my brother.'

'What bet?' He was instantly amused.

'He knew I was mad when I got here. He told me if I stuck this out to the end, I could send him and Jess on any terrible holiday next year and they would go.' She tapped the side of her head. 'You have no idea what I was conjuring up for them.'

'But you'll definitely be making it to the end,' he said. 'You can still be wicked.'

She tilted her head to the side. 'In theory, yes, but in reality? We both meant making it to the end without bailing on the love boat activities, and the truth is, we never really got involved in them, did we?'

Vittorio pulled a face. 'Probably not. The speed dating nearly finished me.'

She laughed. 'Me too!'

Sydney glanced outside the car to the restaurant. 'Are you taking me someplace fancy?'

'Fancy?' It was as if it took him a few moments to translate the meaning. 'If a Michelin star suits you, then yes.'

'Do we have time?'

He nodded. 'Because of all the changes, we have a late departure time tonight, so we can do dinner.'

He opened the door and held out his hand towards her. She stepped out into the warm Monaco air and closed her eyes for a second.

After a moment, he squeezed her hand. 'What is it?'

She kept her eyes closed. 'I'm just following some advice I was given a long time ago, and then again today.'

'What's that?'

She inhaled deeply and looked him square in the eye. 'About living my life, and about what I want in the next five years.'

His look was solemn, but hopeful. There were still so many big conversations to have. But knowing that they were both on the same page was enough for now.

'Is this something we can plan together?'

She gave a slow nod of her head. 'Oh, I think so.' She squeezed his hand as she led him up the steps to the restaurant. She turned her head and raised her eyebrows as they reached the door. 'You know, some people might call me difficult.'

He gave a mock gasp. 'You? Never.' Then he pulled her back for another kiss. 'But know what? I think I'll take the chance.'

CHAPTER TEN

THE PHOTOS AND Instagram reels hit the news in all the wrong way.

It was like the *Minerva* exploded everywhere. There were several couples on the boat who were hitting headlines. A few had real conflict-laden relationships. Another few were emerging as perfect matches and making the whole world sigh. A few others were termed publicity seekers and thought to be fakes, trying to cash in on the hype.

Then there was Sydney and Vittorio.

There was a lot of faraway footage of them. It showed the true nature of their relationship. The heightening attraction, the laughter, the teasing, the chats, and their adventure seeking around the ports. Then there were a few reels, shots of them kissing, interacting together, and exchanging glances, all shot without their knowledge.

Jen looked pale as she came to Vittorio's cabin. Sydney was curled up on top of his bed reading a book.

'What's wrong?' Vittorio asked, taking one look at Jen's face.

She looked distinctly uncomfortable. 'It's not that anything is officially wrong,' she said. 'It's just some things might look as though they are being misinterpreted.'

He frowned. 'What do you mean?'

Sydney leaned over and picked up a tablet, checking out the gossip sites. 'Ouch,' she said out loud.

Jen cringed.

'What is it?' asked Vittorio again.

'Apparently we're both liars and everything about us is fake.' Sydney's voice came out a little funny.

Vittorio swallowed and shook his head. 'Where is this coming from?'

'Reels they've shot of us.' Sydney turned the tablet around so he could see it.

He sat for a few moments and watched them both. They might have made him cringe a little too.

In one clip, Sydney rolled her eyes at him. He knew it was in good humour. But that wasn't apparent when viewed from afar. In another, he was scrolling on his phone as she was talking to him. It looked like he was purposely ignoring her—which of course he hadn't been; he'd been trying to book them dinner in Rome.

But someone, somewhere had decided they were a pair of fakers. Which, in fact, they actually were—just not the way most people thought.

Jen cut in. 'But the whole point of the publicity is to show people that this idea can actually work.' She took a breath. 'Now social media is saying everything is a sham. That we've paid you—' she pointed at them both '—and the rest of the people being interviewed to fake relationships or attractions. They think the shots of you in the restaurants or at the resorts are all just gameplay.'

'Instead of two people getting to know each other gradually and finding out that they like each other?' He chose his words carefully, wondering how Sydney might react.

Jen threw up her hands. 'It's these unauthorised reels that are the problem.'

Vittorio shook his head. 'If you filmed a person all day, you would see a hundred of these moments. They mean nothing. They likely have just as many moments showing us smiling and looking at each other, they've just decided not to show them, because it doesn't fit the narrative. What exactly do you suggest?'

Jen had a momentary look of panic of her face. 'What if we arrange interviews for you both?'

'No.' Their answer was unanimous.

Sydney stood up and walked over to Jen. She

didn't seem to care that she was dressed only a luxurious white towelling gown. 'You already know I don't want to be here. You knew that from the start. You certainly can't demand that I reveal my heart to perfect strangers and the world, just because it suits your agenda.' Her voice was steady, but steely. He could tell she was more than a little annoyed.

Jen's face crumpled. 'That's not what I'm saying. I'm just saying…' Her voice trailed off.

'What?' Vittorio said, wanting to take charge of this uncomfortable situation.

Jen stared out the window at the horizon. 'I'm just saying that things had gone so well. Everyone has loved following the relationships on board. Having people now infer that everything has been faked is disastrous for us.'

Vittorio and Sydney exchanged a glance. Both knew what the other was thinking. This had been fake. It had been intentional. And they'd both agreed to it. But somewhere along the line, something had changed between them.

His stomach plummeted. This cruise company was everything to him. He'd invested his heart and soul. He'd stayed on board to ensure the *Minerva*'s maiden voyage was a success. Now it seemed as though he shouldn't have bothered.

But none of this conflicted as much as his feelings for Sydney. There was so much noise on social media these days that he'd thought the fact that the photographers had been here to snap photos would be enough publicity for them.

He hadn't really thought about all the nuance around it. How some people could infer something and, ten thousand follows later, a mere idea could become fact. The Instagram reels were unfortunate, but they had no control over them.

Because the truth was, if he could, he would tell the world how he felt about Sydney. But now, her initial reaction was making him question his emotions. Maybe she didn't really feel the same as he did. Maybe this was all just a convenience to her, to pass the time for two weeks on her unexpected holiday.

But then he remembered her breath on his skin, the feel of her next to him, the expression in her eyes in Pompeii, Rome, and Monte Carlo. He hadn't imagined that. He hadn't imagined the conversations they'd had.

This was just terrible timing.

'We'll have a chat,' he said to Jen. 'We'll see if we can come up with any ideas.'

Jen could clearly sense the atmosphere in the room. 'Whatever you think,' she said quickly, and headed out the door.

'I don't want my life played out for the world,' Sydney said once the door closed.

He gave a nod of his head, wondering how

best to deal with this, because he did feel the same way. 'We allowed ourselves to be photographed.'

'That was from a distance. That's different. If you agree to more—like giving an interview—it could haunt you forever.'

They looked at each other. 'Only if you don't mean what you say,' he added slowly.

She shifted on her feet but this time wouldn't meet his gaze. 'I've had enough let downs in this life. I couldn't take it if this turned out to be one too—only under the gaze of the world.'

Vittorio stood up and made his way over to her, putting his hands on her upper arms. 'I'm not going to let you down,' he said softly to Sydney, catching her curls with one hand and moving closer to her.

She still wasn't looking at him. It was as if she were afraid to believe him.

'We agreed to fake date, but things have changed.'

'They have,' she agreed, her voice a little shaky. 'But I don't want the world to know about our arrangement. I don't want them to think this is fake now.'

He stroked a finger down her face. 'If you want me to declare that I love you to the world, I will,' he said.

That brought her eyes back to his with a jolt. 'What?'

He gave her a soft smile. 'If you want me to declare that I love you to the world, I will,' he reiterated. 'Because I do.'

He sensed her starting to shake and slid his hands down to her waist. 'I know how I feel about you, Sydney. Yes, it's sudden. Yes, it's unexpected. But I can't pretend it's not there. I know how I feel.'

She licked her lips, her mouth slightly open, as if she were struggling to take in a breath. 'I feel the same,' she admitted.

He couldn't pretend that it didn't feel like his heart was soaring in his chest. If it could have taken off right now, it would have.

He bent to kiss her, tasting her sweet lips and inhaling the scent of oranges from the shower wash in the bathroom. It was his favourite out of the hundreds they'd sampled for the executive suites.

Her hands slid around his neck, pulling them even closer, muscles against the curve of her hips and breasts. The next port might have to wait.

But Sydney pulled back and looked at him. 'If you do that—' she paused '—it might backfire. They might think you're faking that too.'

He blinked. And he knew, just knew, that the thought had charted somewhere in her brain. He couldn't help the well of sadness deep down inside. That—even for a millisecond—she might think that of him, that he might fake his feelings for the sake of his company.

He lifted one of her hands and put it on his chest. 'I would never lie about how I feel about you.' He took another breath. 'And I think you know that.'

She stood for a few moments, watching him. Then shook her head. 'Do what you think is best. But I don't want to be interviewed. They can just photograph us from afar.'

He gave a nod of his head. It wasn't fair to expect Sydney to agree to anything. She hadn't asked to be part of all this and had accepted the requests better than others might have.

He kissed her again, then went to change. He might as well get this part over with before he had too much time to think about it.

'Thanks for speaking to us again. For guests just joining us, this is Vittorio Conti, Chief Executive of Feruli Cruises.'

Vittorio gave a nod of his head. He didn't like the interviewer much and just wanted this over and done with. It was like people on social media were currently rewriting his life history. His *and* Sydney's. He'd read so much nonsense in the past hour it made him want to laugh out loud.

But the sad thing was some people actually believed it, and then repeated the nonsense while adding their own spin to things. So far Sydney had a whole host of careers that weren't actually hers, and had dated a US baseball star, an award-nominated film actor, and her professor at university. Some student had sent a message saying Sydney had been nasty to her on a dig, which had gone viral. Around five minutes of digging showed that Sydney had reprimanded her for not treating the artefacts with the respect they were due—the girl had been caught juggling the artefacts for an Instagram reel.

They'd also dug out his past history, and Alona's name was being bandied around again, along with the veiled allegations.

All reasons Vittorio wanted to set the record straight and get back out of here.

'Vittorio, isn't it unusual for someone in your position to take part in these love games? And have you done it for the publicity for your maiden voyage?'

He was conscious if he showed his true state, he would be snarling right now, so he pasted a smile on his face. 'It's highly unusual for a chief executive to be involved at this level, however, you'll all remember the flight disruptions caused by the volcanic ash. This coincided with the expected arrivals of some of our guests, and we knew that they wouldn't make it to port in time. I was asked to make up the numbers to allow the planned activities to take place, so of course I did.'

'So, you agreed to this?'

He nodded. 'I did. We wanted the maiden voyage to go smoothly with no issues for the guests. Most of them signed up knowing there would be dating activities on board, and we had expectations to fulfil.'

'And is that true of Sydney? Did she come on the boat looking for love?'

Darn it. Vittorio cleared his throat to buy himself a few seconds. 'I believe her brother booked her a holiday as a surprise. She didn't know about the activities until she was on board.'

'So, what attracted you to her?'

Now he wanted to laugh out loud. 'Sydney? Have you seen her? Have you spoken to her? She's a fantastic, accomplished woman with her own mind and a passion for her work. What's not to like?'

The interviewer looked a bit annoyed by that response. 'So, she wasn't just a convenience?'

'Excuse me?'

'Someone you could use to whip up some publicity for the *Minerva*. Is it true not all cabins were sold?'

He blinked. 'No, not at all. She's not a convenience. And, let me assure you, all the cabins were sold.' He held up one hand. 'But not every cabin is occupied due to the flight issues.'

'You weren't dating before this event?'

'I haven't dated for some time.' He wasn't giving them any more than that.

'So, how has this whole thing worked? How did you first meet Sydney?'

'I met her at the first speed-dating event.'

'And did you pair up with her for the port day visit?'

'I've paired up with her for *every* port day visit.' He said the words decisively because his intention was to get this over with as quickly as possible. 'Because I like her. Sydney Scott is a fantastic woman who I'm getting to know. And once this cruise is over, my intention is to get to know her even better.'

The interviewer looked slightly more appeased. Maybe that would be a good sound bite for him. But it was clear the guy was wanting more.

'What do you think the attraction is for Sydney? Is it the fact you're the chief executive of a cruise company, or is it just your Italian charm?'

Vittorio had a flash behind his eyes. It was a tiny spark in his brain where he gave this smarmy interviewer such a shove, he landed on top of the crystal-filled stairs in the atrium. But of course, that didn't happen. Because Vittorio knew when someone was goading him for a reaction.

'You'd need to ask Sydney that. I can't speak on her behalf.'

The guy pressed his lips together.

'Some people have suggested that what you are both doing is fake, to gain headlines for the cruise.'

Vittorio held out both his hands. 'I don't need to create headlines for the *Minerva*. I'm sure that a ship of this class can make headlines of her own. As for our relationship being fake? I can assure you that it is not. What people are seeing when we are together is real.' He shot the guy a slightly disparaging look. 'Maybe you've not seen enough life yet, because when you know, you know.'

He gave his best charming Italian smile at that point and stood up, giving a courteous nod to the camera before leaving.

Jen had been hovering around in the background. But he hadn't been watching her. He didn't need to see every flinch of her face as she contemplated every single word that he said. He would deal with all that later.

His phone buzzed in his pocket again, and he took it out. A number he didn't recognise. He paused for a moment, considering it, before sliding it back into his pocket and heading back to Sydney.

Their next scheduled stop was Barcelona, and he wanted to make sure he was prepared.

Sydney had gone back to her own cabin and was sorting through her clothes. She'd made the mistake of going back online earlier, and it had started to plant bad seeds on her brain. It didn't matter that *she* knew what was true and what wasn't, if enough people said something… She was sure there was actual research somewhere about planting stories in people's brains so often that they started to believe them, and the last thing she wanted was to be a victim of that.

She touched the navy jumper she'd pulled on to walk down the corridor and instantly got a wave of his aftershave. She was falling. She was falling hard.

Sydney Scott didn't do things by half. And even though she hadn't had much luck before, she wanted to be lucky now. It had nothing to do with age, or settling down, or wanting kids, or any of the other nonsense things she'd read about herself online. It had completely and utterly everything to do with Vittorio.

He'd promised not to break her trust, or her heart, in Monte Carlo. Then he'd told her today he would tell the world that he loved her.

And that meant everything. Because Sydney knew that she loved him too.

She could try to pretend it had snuck up on her so slowly and gradually she hadn't realised. But anyone who looked at their time frame would know that to be an absolute lie.

Loving Vittorio Conti had hit her like a thunderbolt. One that still had her reeling.

She hadn't really had time to sit down and think things through. How on earth would they make this work? She still had to go back home and sort out her mother's house, then decide where she would make home. A picture of her mum floated into her head. Maybe this was why all this had happened.

If she'd agreed to sell the house with Peter straight away, she might now have a house or flat in a country or city that wouldn't suit her new long-term relationship. Maybe her mum had actually been watching her from above and telling her to take her time.

She smiled at that, just as Vittorio knocked on her door.

He was beaming. 'Interview finished. Let's make plans for tomorrow.'

'For Barcelona?' She gave him a suspicious smile. 'What do you have in store?'

'It has to be the Sagrada Familia and Montjuïc Castle. And everything Gaudi, of course.'

She smiled and gave him a wary look. 'And here I was thinking I would spend all day touring a certain football stadium.'

He rolled his eyes. 'As if.' Then he leaned forward and whispered in her ear, 'Not this time, but maybe next time, okay?'

She slipped her arms around his neck. 'Okay, but you have to pay a penalty fine.'

His eyes widened in surprise, but his smile told her he knew exactly what she meant. 'And what's that?'

She stood on her tiptoes and whispered in his ear, and he gave a quiet nod, slid his hand into hers, and pulled her towards the bedroom.

CHAPTER ELEVEN

WHEN HIS PHONE went off in the middle of the night with a call from another unknown number, Vittorio nearly didn't answer. But he didn't want the phone to keep going and wake Sydney, so he did.

He didn't recognise the voice, but he immediately heard the anxiety. It made him swing his legs out of bed and take a couple of steps away. He listened for a few more moments, his heart sinking.

His mind was reeling. But his strong moral fibre was etched into his very being. He grabbed some clothes, knowing he couldn't do anything further without talking to Sydney.

He gave her a shake and she groaned. 'I need to go and deal with something,' he said. 'I'm sorry, I'll be back, I promise.' She grunted, and he gave her a shake again. He'd much rather have a proper chat, but it was the middle of the night, and she'd complained of a headache earlier, so was it fair to wake her when he didn't know all the details?

He'd leave another message with Javier. Right now, he had to deal with something he'd helped create.

When Sydney woke, she was surprised the bed next to her was empty. Javier appeared with breakfast for her, saying that Vittorio had gone to deal with an emergency and would be in touch. There weren't many more details, though she had a vague memory of him shaking her in the middle of the night.

She kept the blinds closed as she ate, the headache from last night still dully present. She was praying it wouldn't turn into a migraine. She'd only had two in her life. The first one had landed her in hospital, and the second her local doctor had dealt with by giving her an injection and making her lie in darkness for nearly a full twenty-four hours. It was the aura that had been the worst part. The flickering lights, the altered vision—she really didn't want to go down that road again.

So she took it easy, eating, showering, and dressing with a large brimmed hat and dark glasses, before finally making her way to the disembarkation point where she hoped Vittorio might be waiting for her.

He wasn't.

In a way she was glad, she wasn't sure she could face Barcelona today. She stood on the deck for a few moments, looking out at the city she would likely miss, and then went to find Jen, but the corridors and stairwell were busy, and she couldn't stand the noise so she went back to her room to lie down again.

She took what medication she had and thought about calling the on-board doctor.

Four hours later, when she woke with the aura glistening around her, she knew she had to. He attended quickly, took her history and gave her an injection similar to she'd had before. She asked the doctor if he would send a message to Vittorio for her, and he immediately agreed.

When she woke again it was night and she was a little surprised Vittorio wasn't there. There was some fruit and water on a nearby table with a note from Javier saying that Vittorio would be in touch. What did that mean? Where was he?

Jen appeared looking pensive. 'Where is Vittorio?' she asked.

Jen bit her lip. 'He had to leave the boat in the middle of the night. It was an emergency. He said he would call you.'

'He's left the boat?' Now she was surprised. What emergency had meant he had to leave the boat? Then she frowned. 'How did he get off?'

'Helicopter,' said Jen, her face completely straight. 'I haven't heard from him either.' It was like she said that to try to placate Sydney. 'Are you feeling better? The doctor wanted to check on you again when you woke.'

Sydney gave a nod of her head. 'I'm fine. I'm just a bit groggy.'

Jen gave a smile and disappeared out the cabin.

So Sydney waited, and waited, and waited. She tried to call his number, but it wouldn't connect.

She had dinner in the cabin and spent a restless night. By the next day, the fog in her brain had entirely lifted and she was determined to get to the bottom of what was going on. She'd just dressed again when there was a knock at her door. Javier looked at her apologetically. 'You have some guests.'

Jim and Mary were standing behind him and she ushered them in. Mary was shifting from foot to foot and Jim was twisting his hands together. She waited until Javier left and sat down with them at the table.

'Are you okay?' said Mary gently, putting her hand on Sydney's arm.

A chill ran through her. 'Why wouldn't I be okay?'

The elderly couple exchanged a glance. Jim took a breath. 'Vittorio, he's in the news.'

'What do you mean?'

Mary gestured to the tablet sitting on her table. 'Take a look.'

Sydney hadn't touched social media. She had no use for it, and had certainly not looked at a screen while she'd been in the depths of her migraine.

She searched Vittorio's name, and a huge range of headlines appeared. The first showed a picture of her with the title *High and Dry.*

Her blood ran cold. It was a photo of her leaning on the railing, looking out at Barcelona with her dark glasses and large hat on. But it was the photo underneath that cut to the bone.

Vittorio, holding up a thin blonde woman, and taking her inside a building.

Sydney knew immediately who it was. Alona. The supermodel he used to date.

Her heart stopped.

He'd told her to trust him. He'd told her that her heart was safe with him. They were looking to the future, to what might come next. And now…this?

Sydney couldn't catch her breath. Jim and Mary were still looking at her. She blinked and just held up her hands. 'I guess once a fool, always a fool.'

Jim stood up, looking for all intents and purposes as if he might punch someone on her behalf. It gave her an age-old memory of her father and warmed her ice-cold heart.

She put her hand on his arm. 'Can you do me a favour?'

'Anything,' he said, and she believed him.

'Can you make arrangements for me to leave the boat before it leaves port today?'

She didn't even know which port they were currently in, and she cared even less. Once she was onshore, she would find a flight to…somewhere.

Her phone started to ring as she opened her cupboards and started throwing clothing into her suitcases. She glanced at it once—Vittorio.

It only made her more determined. Mary stepped up next to her and helped with her packing, stopping her harum-scarum way of throwing everything in. Sydney had to lean on the first suitcase to get it to close, but Jim had returned at that point with a determined look on his face and some elderly muscle to grab her cases for her. 'I've got a taxi waiting for you at the port gates.'

'Did you have any problems?'

'None that I couldn't sort. Come on.'

He waved Javier away, as he wanted to carry the cases, and walked her down to the disembarkation point, Mary trotting behind them.

Jen appeared out of nowhere. 'Sydney!' she shouted, waving her hand.

Sydney's phone started again, and she looked. Peter. She felt herself start to wobble. Life was about to come tumbling down on her again, just like it had a few years ago. Last time she'd lost her mum. This time she was losing the person she loved and being humiliated in front of the world. Would she lose her job? Her university position? Her chance at leading a dig?

She scanned her card to leave the boat and hugged both Mary and Jim. 'Thank you so much, I appreciate you coming to see me this morning.'

'I'll have words with him,' growled Jim.

'I doubt he'll be back,' said Sydney as the realisation started to hit even harder.

A crew member took her suitcases down the ramp for her, and she answered her phone. 'Pete,' was all she managed before she started to cry.

From the second he'd been helicoptered from the boat, everything that could go wrong, had gone wrong—including the headlines.

It turned out the anonymous calls had been from Alona's agent, who'd watched her spiralling over a number of days. She'd apparently been unwell for a while, and the recent news around Vittorio and Sydney had sunk her into a depression.

By the time he'd finally got a hold of Vittorio, Alona was threatening suicide unless she could speak to Vittorio again.

Vittorio knew she was fragile. Knew that her addictions had once again taken hold. He also knew he wasn't the answer to this, and that he was responsible for it, but that didn't allow his heart and brain to come together. If one conversation with him could help put someone he'd once loved back on track, then he could do that.

And then the world had exploded.

He'd reached the hotel she'd barricaded herself inside. Even though the agent was trying to keep everything under the media's radar, someone had leaked that he was there. Alona was extremely unwell. She'd held on to him and sobbed. It didn't matter she'd dated a number of other men since they'd split. She didn't want him to love anyone else.

Vittorio had been very honest. He'd told her he would always care about her, and would always help her if he was in a position to do so, but that he'd met someone else now, and he loved her.

Alona had been silent, and had finally agreed to see the doctor that her agent had pleaded with her to see for months.

She'd asked Vittorio to go with her, and he'd agreed. She'd finally been admitted to a private hospital. Her agent had said that Alona had funds to cover it, but Vittorio had insisted on covering the costs until she was well enough to make decisions for herself again.

Then he'd tried to contact Sydney, only to be told she was unwell and being seen by the ship's doctor. He'd been frantic but had been caught between a rock and a hard place. The doctor—rightly—wouldn't tell him anything.

He'd tried to call her on her mobile, but the call wouldn't connect.

He'd contacted Jen to leave messages, only to find out Sydney was planning on leaving. He'd tried to contact her again, but she hadn't answered. He'd left message after message, and by the time he made it back to the ship, she was gone.

Then he'd seen the headlines, and his heart had plummeted to the bottom of the sea. He knew what those headlines would have meant to her. He understood why she hadn't answered her phone. She'd thought his promises false, his words about planning for a future all something to keep her happy while on board.

By the time he'd reached the ship, the initial headlines had morphed into something even worse: That it had all been a publicity ploy for the company. Sydney Scott had been played while Vittorio Conti and Alona had never actually split at all and had been dating in secret for the past eighteen months. There was even speculation that Alona had hidden away to hide a pregnancy and have their baby.

All complete and utter nonsense. All designed to break Sydney Scott's heart.

And he was at the centre of it all.

CHAPTER TWELVE

As soon as she set foot in the house, she just let go. Of everything. The familiar scent hit her straight away. The cleaning products her mother had used, the faint aroma of her perfume still hanging there, after all this time. The smells from the garden that she'd known all her life were there too.

And once Peter had dropped her off and left, she just lay down on the sofa and sobbed.

Everything had just got too much for her. The betrayal, the bereavement, the sole focus on her work at the expense of all other aspects of her life. There was so much she hadn't given herself time to think about. And now, it seemed like she finally had time.

Her phone had kept ringing. Vittorio was persistent. He'd left message after message. But she wasn't interested. She hadn't listened to a single one of them and eventually blocked his number.

After a day or so, she finally took a breath to look around. Tiny filaments of dust had gathered around the house. It had been empty for over eighteen months, and no matter where she might be in her life, she knew it was finally time to put things in order.

She called Peter, and they spent the next two days collecting keepsakes, making runs to various charity shops, and donating clothes and household items where they were needed.

Some of the furniture was too old to be donated due to new fire safety rules, so after a discussion with an estate agent it was decided to leave it for now. The estate agent said that completely empty houses tended to put people off, and a house with at least some furniture in it would likely sell better.

The pictures were taken and the house was listed. Sydney had no idea how quickly it would sell. She still hadn't decided on her next move, but she would be going back to Egypt soon, and she already had a rental premises there. Long-term decisions could be made later.

Peter tried to pin her down on what had happened. He'd seen Vittorio in the news and kept trying to talk to her about it. But she just held up her hand and said it wasn't open for discussion.

She hadn't done another online search since the original one. She had no wish to know how the reignited romance had progressed. She wasn't interested in the consequences for Vittorio's company. She'd spoken to Josef, who'd told her everything at the dig was fine, and to come back when she was ready.

Flowers started arriving at the house. Large bouquets, filled with beautiful, fragrant blooms, most of which she didn't recognise. One set was given to Peter for Jess, another to a neighbour. Another to her favourite baker in town, who made the most delectable chocolate eclairs. Sydney didn't read the notes—she just binned them.

By the time the fourth bouquet arrived, along with a hamper from somewhere that she didn't even open, the delivery driver was intrigued. 'Take that back with you,' she said, gesturing to the hamper.

'What? Have you any idea how much that's worth?'

'I don't care,' she said. 'And you'll be doing me a favour if you take it. Someone is booked to view the house tonight and I don't want it cluttering up the place.'

The driver looked sceptical.

'Take the flowers too.'

He shook his head. 'Brenda at the flower shop had to specially order those blooms. If someone is coming to view the house, won't a nice bouquet of flowers look welcoming? Make the place smell nice?'

Sydney stopped for a second and considered

his words. 'Okay, leave the flowers, but take the hamper, please.'

The guy nodded and disappeared while she carried the flowers into the house. He'd been right. The smell was beautiful and drifted around the house.

She was nervous. She'd never listed a house before, or shown viewers around. Most people—especially the nosey ones—just looked at the listing online. The estate agent had said they would come and meet her before the appointment, and five minutes later, she pulled up.

Jane had been very professional, but as she came in, she looked a little flustered. 'What's wrong?' asked Sydney. 'Has the viewer pulled out?' She'd heard about this happening to other people.

Jane shook her head. 'No, it's something different…they've put in an offer.'

'Before they've seen the house?'

Jane nodded. 'It's quite unusual, and not only that, it's a substantial offer, well over the asking price.'

'Why would anyone do that?'

Jane shrugged. 'I'm not sure. Maybe it's someone who is desperate to move into the area? Or has set their sights on a house with a garden and stream like yours. Honestly? I have no idea.'

Jane started to walk through the house again,

checking everything was ready. She'd given Sydney some tips on what to do before the walk-through and now stopped at the flowers. 'Oh, these are beautiful. What a nice touch.'

'You can take them once the viewing is over,' Sydney said quickly. 'I won't be keeping them.'

The stones of the gravel driveway crunched, signalling a car pulling up. A minute later, there was a knock at the door.

Sydney answered, and stopped dead.

Vittorio stood on her doorstep.

Her first reaction was to slam the door in his face, but Jane rushed over to welcome him in. 'Mr Conti, I'm so pleased that you've made it. I was just telling Ms Scott that you've made an offer on the property.'

Sydney turned and walked away. 'The property isn't for sale. Mr Conti and I have history, and I can't—and won't—be bought.'

Vittorio had followed them both into the house, catching sight of the bouquet. He gave a small smile.

Jane looked confused. 'I'm sorry, what?'

Vittorio dipped his head. 'I'm sorry, Jane. Ms Scott and I do have history, but the offer on the house does stand. I want to buy it.'

Jane looked from one to the other, then touched Sydney on the arm. 'I'm thinking this is a conversation I shouldn't be part of. But Sydney, is there a safety issue here? Or can I leave you two alone to talk?'

Sydney let out a huge sigh, glanced at Vittorio, then looked back at Jane. 'There's no safety issue.'

Jane looked between them both again and said in a steady voice, 'In that case, I'll leave you two alone. Give me a call later, Sydney.'

They both waited until Jane left and they heard the crunch of her tires on the drive.

'That wasn't fair, you shouldn't have done that,' said Sydney promptly. She was trying to ignore the wave of emotions that had washed over her the moment she'd glimpsed his face.

'You're a hard woman to get in contact with. It seemed the best solution,' he said in a low voice.

She folded her arms. 'Maybe you should take a hint. I haven't listened to any of your messages.' The anger still burned deep inside.

Vittorio looked around the house, and then walked over and sat down on the sofa. 'I came to talk, Sydney, and I'm not leaving until we've had that chance.'

She was immediately indignant. 'This is my home. How dare you? I don't want to talk, Vittorio. If I did—don't you think I would have answered one of your messages?'

'That you didn't listen to?' was his immediate response.

She closed her eyes for a second. 'I didn't need, or want, to be a pawn in this game. Go back to Alona—that is, if you ever really left her. But you didn't need to humiliate me in front of the world. If you'd had any respect for me, you would never have done that. I need you to leave.'

Vittorio put his head in his hands for a moment, and she chose to continue.

'I hope you got all the publicity for your ship that you needed. I hope that your sales are through the roof. Actually, I don't hope any of those things, because I don't like to be used. You fooled me, Vittorio. I won't be your victim again.'

He lifted his head, and his brown eyes connected with hers. The expression on his face was pure pain, and for a second she was confused. What did he have to be hurt about?

He stood up and moved next to her. 'Alona is unwell. Really unwell. She has addiction and mental health problems. I had missed calls on my phone for days—all from unfamiliar numbers—and when I finally answered, it was her agent. She was threatening suicide unless I went to see her and speak to her. She was holed up in a hotel in Paris and the police were involved.'

Sydney looked at him, not quite sure what to say. This was all news to her.

'So, when I got the call, I went. I'm sorry I

didn't fully wake you to tell you what was going on. And when I got there, the police were controlling the situation and asked everyone to turn off all mobile devices until the situation was resolved.'

'And is it?'

He closed his eyes for a second. 'She's sick, and she's someone I used to care about. Someone I used to love.' He took a moment and looked at Sydney. 'She asked me about you. She'd seen all the news reports about us, and that was what tipped her. She hadn't been well for a long time, and if it hadn't been reports about us, it would likely have been something else.'

'What does that mean?' Sydney said, starting to get frustrated by all this.

He touched her arm. 'I told her the truth. I told her that I'd met someone that I love and I want to be with.'

Sydney's eyes widened. 'Are you allowed to say that to someone who is suicidal?'

He spoke quietly. 'Alona is unwell. I recognise some parts of her illness. I can't give her any false belief. I had to be honest with her. I told her what you meant to me, but I also told her I would continue to support her if she wanted.'

Sydney looked at the hand touching her arm. What did all this actually mean? Was he suggesting that they share him?

She shook her head, not quite sure what words should come out.

Vittorio continued. 'I've paid for her to spend time at an addiction clinic. I'm in contact with her agent, but that's it. I've made it clear that I was happy to help on a one-off occasion, but I won't let her emotionally manipulate me. She needs to have supportive friends and family around her—and she does, she just cut herself off from them while she was unwell. Her doctors agree.'

'So…the picture?'

'The picture was of me helping her to the car.'

'Shouldn't the police have done that if they were there?'

'It was agreed to try to keep the fuss to a minimum. The press was already there. The arrangements had been made for the clinic, and the doctors agreed that her agent and I could transport her there.'

Sydney still didn't speak. She was trying to take everything in.

'I would have explained all this to you, but when I got back to the ship, you were already gone.' He gave her a sad smile. 'And Jim was waiting to tell me what he thought of me.'

He ran his hand along her arm and took both her hands.

'But, Sydney, I feel as if Alona is the elephant

in the room. Please talk to me about all this. You ran away. You ran away from me. Don't you want us to be together? Don't you love me the way that I love you?'

He moved them both back to the sofa, and this time Sydney allowed herself to sit down.

Her voice was caught in her throat, because she knew he'd hit the nail on the head. She'd allowed herself to be swept up in the social media stories. She'd let herself believe them, rather than taking time to wait, and asking herself if she truly thought Vittorio would do something like that to her. She could have answered her phone, but she'd chosen not to. Why?

Tears sprang to her eyes. 'That's just it, I can't take this. You knew I'd had my heart broken before, and I couldn't take it again. This is exactly what I didn't want to happen—and you did this. You did this to me in front of the world. I loved you, Vittorio, and you treated me like nothing. Do you have any idea what that feels like?'

He pulled back from her, clearly surprised at the anguish and venom in her words. Hot tears spilled down her face. The rage that had burned inside had just erupted, and now it was out, she didn't want to stop.

'Do you know how much that hurt? How hard it was to hold it together? Pictures splashed everywhere telling the world I was High and Dry.

A laughing stock. Is it any wonder I didn't want to speak to you?'

His eyes were wide and he tried to speak, but she put her hand up to stop him.

'Look around. This was my mum's house. She died eighteen months ago, and the truth is, I couldn't deal with it. Any of it. And I just ran back to Egypt to duck away and hide my heart from any of it. I can't do this, Vittorio. I can't do any of this.'

He reached out and took both her hands. Tears were pouring down his face too. 'I'm sorry, I'm so, so sorry. But I was honest about how I felt about you. I love you, Sydney. And I want to spend the rest of my life with you. I don't want a life without you in it. I'm sorry I've complicated things. I had to help when asked. That's just me. That's just the person I am. And I hope that deep down, you know that. But trust me when I say that I love you.' He shook his head. 'You haven't checked the news, have you?'

She shook her head.

'Well, my company stock soared, plummeted, and soared again.'

She let out a short laugh. 'So, this is all just to have more good publicity for your company?'

'My company is soaring right now, but it doesn't mean anything, because social media seems to turn on a dime. I've read more stories about you and me in the last few days than I thought possible to write—or more accurately, make up. You should know that apparently you were dating a world-famous movie star before me, and have been secretly married and have three hidden children.'

'What?'

He nodded. 'The sad part is that no one really knows the truth because they're not interested in the truth. They don't know about Alona's addiction or relapse, or where she is now. And I won't tell. I won't break the confidence of someone who is already broken. Who doesn't need to be headlines in a paper for a few days, and then forgotten about. They think I plotted all of this.' He held up his hands. 'How could anyone? Even the best thriller writer couldn't have predicted all our twists and turns.' He took a moment to collect himself. 'I've loved the cruise business. I've invested my whole life in it. Social media is a game I've never played and that's clear, because I had no idea how intrusive and vicious they could be. I want to protect you. I want to protect us from all this.' He looked at her pleadingly. 'Because I don't care how well my company is doing if I don't have you in my life.' He stared out the window. 'I never imagined I would meet someone on the cruise and fall in love. But it happened.' He reached out to touch her face, 'It happened with you. And I can't predict our future. I can't tell you how we can make our lives work between Italy and Egypt. But my heart tells me I don't want to go on without you. I want to have a future with you in it. With you by my side.'

'But how can I know that any of this is real? No one knew this all started as a joke—a deal between the two of us to fake date. And now? We were called on it, Vittorio. Somebody, somewhere in the world called us on the fact we'd planned to fake it all. And even now, I'm questioning things. I'm wondering if I played into this plan for publicity, even more so by believing in things myself. I feel as if I can't trust my feelings or my judgement. I haven't made good decisions in the past—so what on earth makes me think I can make a good decision now?'

She could see the pain on his face. She knew her words had hurt him.

He reached over and put a hand on her chest. 'Because you have to listen to what's in here. I know that you love me, just as much as I love you. I know because I've been there. I've been there for every word, every interaction. I've felt it, just like you have. This is not fake. This is real. Every part of this is real. How can you doubt it?'

A tear slid down her cheek as she looked at

his hand, but she didn't remove it. 'This is all so much. I don't know if I can believe it all.'

He gave a sad smile. 'Ask your brother. I've spent the past two days persuading him to let me come after you. He's a hard guy to win round. He and his wife would fight to the death for you. You have an amazing family.' He looked around again. 'I wish I'd had the chance to meet your mum.'

She was amazed. 'You've spoken to Peter.'

He nodded. 'I've sat down with him.'

'And what did you tell him?'

'Everything I told you. And that I love his sister and want to spend the rest of my life with her.'

She sat back, knowing exactly how protective Peter and Jess were of her, and exactly how hard a job he would have faced.

'It's all just so…overwhelming.'

He touched her hands again, clasping them in his. 'I know, and I get it. You are more important to me than anything. You said that you loved me earlier. Is it true? Do you love me?'

Her words were barely a whisper. 'Yes.'

'Then come on this journey with me. Let's do it together. Let's find our path together and do it at our own pace.' He smiled around the room. 'Let me buy the house. Let me donate it to that charity you said you wanted to help. What could be nicer for families who need a break than to come to a place like this?'

'You remembered that?'

'Of course I remembered,' he said. He touched her cheek. 'Because everything about you is worth remembering,' he added simply, then gave her a sorry stare. 'I should have protected you from all this. A few years ago, I was at the mercy of the media, and it was part of the reason I stayed away from relationships. I'd thought that time had passed. I'd forgotten that nothing that's been online ever dies. I should never have asked you to fake date. It's all my fault, Sydney. The headlines, the media, I should never have asked you to take part. I should have remembered. And for that, I am so sorry.'

She gave a little smile. 'Well, I was hardly anyone famous to date. To be honest, I didn't expect anyone to be interested—they never have been before. This isn't your fault, Vittorio. I know that.' She gave him a smile with a gleam in her eyes. 'And I look forward to reading which movie star I secretly dated, and where the hidden children are.'

He leaned forward and put both hands on her cheeks, resting his forehead against hers. 'I love you, Sydney Scott, and I promise to keep you and your heart safe from here forwards.'

She blinked back the tears forming. 'I love you

too, Vittorio Conti, and have no problem holding you to that promise from now on.'

'Well, that's lucky,' he said, reaching into his pocket and pulling out something else. He handed it to her, and she opened the slightly crumpled paper, staring at the itinerary.

She gave a little gasp. 'No!'

He smiled. 'You said it was the one place you still wanted to go.'

'You're taking me to see the Terracotta Army?'

He nodded, grinning. 'I am,' he said. 'If you'll go.'

She wrapped her arms around him, smiling broadly. 'That will be a yes.'

And then she kissed him, ready to start her whole new life.

* * * * *